JEREMY AND THE AUNTIES

JEREMY AND THE AUNTIES

by

Felicity Finn

Illustrations by

Sally J.K. Davies

CANADIAN CATALOGUING IN PUBLICATION

Finn, Felicity
Jeremy and the aunties

ISBN 0-929005-40-6

I. Title.

PS8561.I55J4 1992   jC813'.54   C92-094972-X
PZ7.F45Je 1992

*Second Story Press gratefully acknowledges the assistance of the
Ontario Arts Council and the Canada Council*

Printed and bound in Canada

Published by
SECOND STORY PRESS
760 Bathurst Street
Toronto Canada M5S 2R6

For
Allen, Henry, Jesse,
and Brian
with love

CONTENTS

CHAPTER ONE

THE THREE AUNTIES

I WASN'T AFRAID OF THE AUNTIES at first. It was only later, after we'd seated them on the living room couch in front of the TV, just as if they were watching a show, that a little shiver of fear went down my back. They looked so real.

The aunties were my mother's idea. Ever since she'd got her new job as set-designer at the theatre, she had been planning a big celebration. She thought that three stuffed guests at the party would be good for a laugh.

It took us almost a week to make them. First my mother collected everything we needed from second-hand stores, fabric shops, and the theatre costume department, and then we started work. I don't normally sew. But the TV had mysteriously gone on the blink that night so I had nothing better to do.

"You can be in charge of limbs and bodies, Jeremy," my mother said. "I'll take care of the tricky bits, like faces and fingers."

The legs were the easiest. I just stuffed three pairs of pantyhose full of cotton batting and stuck the feet into shoes. The hands and fingers were a bit of a problem. Eventually we stuffed three pairs of gloves and sewed them onto the arms. My mother had a lot of fun with the faces. First she stitched on a nose, ears, a lip line, and eyelids. Then she sewed in wrinkles, dimples, crow's-feet, and creases by the cheeks and mouth. By the time she'd added makeup, wigs, and clothes, the three aunties looked almost alive.

"We must name them, Jeremy," my mother said. "To me they look *exactly* like a Mabel, a Gladys, and a Dotty. What do you think?"

"Sure."

"I fear old Mabel is a bit of a prude." She looked the first doll over with satisfaction.

"I think we made Gladys too fat," I commented.

My mother sighed. "Yes, she really should try to lose a few pounds. And that dress! Obviously poor Gladys has absolutely no taste when it comes to clothes. It looks like she bought her entire outfit at a second-hand store." We giggled.

"Now Dotty's what I call a real doll," my mother said. "I'll bet she broke a few hearts in her day."

They all looked like real dolls to me, sitting there on the couch. So real, in fact, that I half expected them to speak. Another strange shiver ran down my spine.

"Why not invite one of *your* friends tonight, Jeremy?" my mother asked. "Summer holidays have started. One night of wild partying — under my supervision, of course — shouldn't hurt you."

"Okay!" The choice was easy. I went to the phone and called Rick. Rick and I have been best friends all our lives.

He answered the phone in his usual way: "Ricketts here."

"Hey, Rick," I said. "My mother's having a party tonight — all adults — probably boring — but she said I could invite you over. And there's something I want to show you."

"Can't make it," Rick said. "My mother's in town to take me out for dinner. My dad plans to go, though."

"Oh," I said. "Well, come over tomorrow, then. We made something you've got to see."

That night I pretended to go up to bed, but later I crept along the hall and watched everything from the stairs. The aunties stole the show. All my mother's friends loved them. "Charming! So original! So lifelike!" they exclaimed. As we had hoped, some of the guests, when they first entered the room, thought the aunties were real people. I saw one of my mother's co-workers pass a tray of smoked sausages to Gladys, then blush and look around to see if anyone had noticed. By the end of the evening, a slightly tipsy Professor Ricketts was sitting on the couch with his arm around Dotty, deep in conversation with her. Dr. Suggs was waltzing around the room with Mabel and her cane.

The next morning I was downstairs early to watch cartoons. The TV had started working again the night we finished the aunties. I like TV — sports, game shows, comedies, movies, cartoons, reruns, everything — and I'd really missed it. I looked around the living room for leftover treats. I found a few cold sausages, as well as some potato chips and five chocolates on a tray. I was crouched down, reaching under an armchair for a bowl of chip dip, when I thought I heard someone clear her throat. I froze. Then a voice quite near me said, "Imagine, going to bed and leaving all this mess and clutter behind. Didn't even wash the dishes! What kind of a household is this?"

The hairs on my neck bristled up. I scrunched down very small and listened. I heard another, younger, voice reply, "But it was a lovely party, I must say. That Professor Ricketts is *such* a charming conversationalist. So intellectual!"

"Really," snapped the first voice, "I am surprised at you, Dotty. Letting yourself be flattered by that nasty red-faced fellow with wine stains on his shirt.

He was not even wearing a tie. Goodness!"

"Why, Mabel, I declare! I saw you dancing with that handsome doctor and enjoying every minute of it."

"I certainly did not enjoy it, Dotty, my dear. He simply grabbed me and began to waltz. What could I do? I tried my best to kick him in the shins and trip him up with my cane."

"The lady of the house may be a terrible house-keeper," said a third voice, "but she does know how to cook. That food looked good enough to eat. I was afraid all evening that my stomach might start growling."

Slowly, I raised my head over the back of the armchair. There was no one else in the room. No one, that is, except the three aunties, who were sprawled on the couch just as they'd been left the night before. Stuffed dolls cannot speak, I told myself firmly, no matter how real they look. It's impossible. But I shivered with cold, and all the ghost stories I had ever heard crowded into my mind.

Then I almost laughed out loud. Of course! My mother, or some of her crazy friends, rigged this up to entertain me! I searched frantically under the furniture and behind the cushions for the hidden tape recorder. But there was none to be found, not even under the aunties' couch.

My next thought was, Aha! Speakers hidden in their stuffing! My mother must be speaking into a microphone from her room. It would be just like her. Though none of the voices had sounded like hers . . . They were thin and quavery — like the voices of very old ladies.

I approached the aunties a little timidly. I wasn't used to poking around in women's hair and clothing. I began with Mabel. She was the oldest of the three, dressed all in black. I looked under her small hat and veil, and under her grey wig. I checked her cane and the little silver locket around her neck. I squeezed her all over — under her shawl, under her dress. There was no hard bump anywhere. Her little eyes seemed to stare at me with disgust and I finished searching her as quickly as I could.

Dotty was next. She was the youngest and the prettiest of the aunties. She wore a navy blue suit and high-heeled button shoes. There were feathers on her hat, and a fur was tossed over one shoulder. I even checked her beaded handbag and long cigarette holder. Again, no trace of a speaker.

That left only Gladys. Her flowered dress was very tight over her chest, and her feet bulged over her shoes. She wore a sparkly sweater, several rings and necklaces, and huge pearl earrings. She also had a large purse and a flowered umbrella. I started squeezing her chubby arms.

Suddenly she began to giggle uncontrollably. I jerked back my hands in terror. She kept on laughing and hiccupping, and gasped out, "Ooh, I just couldn't help it, I'm so ticklish."

"You're alive!" I gasped, scrambling back out of reach. The scariest thing was that, though the words and giggles sounded just as though they were coming from inside her, her stitched lips hadn't opened.

"Do I look dead?" Gladys giggled. Dotty's shoulders slumped, and Mabel sniffed.

"Now you've done it," Mabel said to Gladys, and turning slightly towards me, she said, "What a dreadful boy you are, going around poking and tickling elderly ladies. Did no one teach you manners?" Her mouth wiggled a little but did not open.

"S-sorry," I stammered, stumbling back a few more steps. "I-I thought you were j-just stuffed dolls."

"Stuffed dolls, indeed!" Mabel sniffed. "You ought to be ashamed of yourself. Now, if you would be so kind, you might help us out of these un-dignified postures."

I hesitated. Though I was shaking a bit, I knew it had to be a trick. I said very loudly, "This is a great conversation, whoever you are, but you haven't tricked me, so why not turn off the microphone and we can talk in person." As I finished speaking, I heard my mother turn on the shower upstairs. That meant she couldn't be making the voices! So the aunties could actually talk all by themselves? Unreal! I approached the couch cautiously and set them up straight, being careful to touch them as little as possible.

"Thank you," said Mabel primly.

"Your name, we understand, is Jeremy?" the auntie named Dotty said in a friendly voice.

I nodded.

"Delightful name. I'm Dotty, and these are my cousins, Mabel and Gladys."

"I-I know," I whispered, holding out my hand to show I did have some manners. None of them took it. I knew they could move a little, enough to shrug or move their fingers. Suddenly I imagined them prowling through the house at night, creeping up the stairs to my room. "Ex-excuse me," I stammered, "b-but I just wondered — I mean — can you walk?"

"Walk?" Gladys snickered. "He wants to know if we can walk."

"Bum leg," Mabel said with dignity, pointing to her cane.

"Of course we can't," said Dotty. "Could you

walk on legs like these?" They exchanged amused glances. "And by the by, my dear Jeremy, since we're exchanging personal information, would you mind telling us, er, where exactly we, er, find ourselves? Address, city, year . . . just out of curiosity."

"Well, this is 269a Oriole Aven —"

I broke off as my mother came down the stairs.

"Hi, Jeremy. Talking to the aunties? They were the life of the party last night! Well, don't let me interrupt your conversation. I'd rather you talked to stuffed dolls than watched mindless cartoons. Have you made breakfast?"

I followed her into the kitchen, and while she made tea and cinnamon toast, I tried to find out just what was going on. Most of the time I get along with my mom pretty well. I can usually talk to her about just about anything.

"Uh, Mom," I began, "uh, you don't believe in ghosts, do you?"

"Certainly I do! All my life I've been dying to meet one — no pun intended. Have you seen one, Jeremy?"

"Mom, have you rigged up the aunties to talk?"

"No — but what a wonderful idea! Why didn't I think of it for the party? Just imagine the effect!" She looked at me. "Why do you ask, Jeremy?"

I knew that if she ever realized exactly what she

had created, she'd be so ecstatic that she'd probably go on making life-sized stuffed dolls until the house was filled up. I could just imagine dozens of wrinkled old creatures — sitting at the table, curled up on the beds, waiting by the phone, soaking in the tub. And all jabbering away at the tops of their lungs! The thought was a little frightening. Pretty horrible, as a matter of fact. Three of them were quite enough for me. "Just joking," I said with a shrug.

My mother went back to her tea, looking disappointed. After breakfast she disappeared upstairs with a book. I couldn't wait till Rick arrived.

CHAPTER TWO

THE END OF A LONG FRIENDSHIP

I WAITED IN THE DRIVEWAY. Rick and I have lots in common. Both of us are interested in tennis and TV, and bored by school and girls. We even look sort of the same, except he's skinnier and doesn't have freckles or glasses. I call him Rick, short for Ricketts, but a lot of the kids at school call him Rich, because he is. The interesting thing about Rick is that he is richer than his father, Professor Ricketts, who he lives with most of the time. Thanks to his mother, who remarried a stockbroker, Rick has a computer, an electric guitar, his own TV and VCR, three Nintendos, and his own phone. He's a good guy to know — rich, popular, *and* smart. Lots of kids wonder why we're friends.

"What's new, Jeremy?" he asked, hopping off his bike.

I smiled mysteriously. It wasn't often that I had something Rick didn't. He was always getting new videos and computer games. But three talking aunties beat even computer games by a mile.

"Have I got a surprise for you!" I led him inside. "You're never going to believe this! It's the most incredible thing — you'll never guess."

"I've got some news too," he said. "But you can go first."

"This is it!" I announced as we walked into the living room. "Take a good look. What do you see?"

Rick glanced around. "I see a fairly messy room that looks like it's recovering from a party, and — what's this? Three stuffed dolls sitting on the couch."

"Right!" I shouted.

"Dad mentioned something about meeting three new old ladies at the party . . ."

"Rick," I said formally, "I'd like you to meet the three aunties, Mabel, Gladys, and Dotty. Mabel, Gladys, and Dotty — my friend Rick."

I expected them to say "How do you do?" or "Pleased to meet you" or something like that. They said absolutely nothing.

"Yeah?" said Rick. "Where did you get them?"

"Mom and I made them for the party."

"*This* is what you wanted to show me?"

"But that's not all! This morning when I came downstairs, I discovered something absolutely radical. You're never going to believe this, Rick, but the aunties can talk!"

"Right."

"Really! They told me their names and everything, and they seem to be able to move a little bit too."

"Sure, Jeremy. I bet I can guess what their names are." He grinned and pointed at Mabel. "This old nasty-looking auntie is probably Auntie Freeze. And this chunky one" — he pointed at Gladys — "looks like Auntie Pasto." He looked at Dotty admiringly. "And I bet this one's Auntie Body, right?" He let out a big laugh.

"Very funny," I said. "It's not very nice to insult people to their faces, you know." I turned to the aunties. "Don't mind him," I said. "Rick's got a weird sense of humour. Um, how are you doing? Looks like a nice day outside today, doesn't it?" I could feel my face getting red. Rick was grinning at me. Suddenly I had a horrible thought. My mother had often told me that I did not have a very developed imagination, but what if she was wrong? What if I had *imagined* my conversation with the aunties?

"Don't you want to hear my news?"

Of course I did.

Rick pulled a crumpled paper from his pocket. "This was on a phone pole downtown. See? REWARD offered for information leading to the arrest of three bank robbers. It gives their names and descriptions. The two of us could have a great time this summer tracking them down. What do you think. Come back to my place and we can feed the information into my computer and get started."

I was tempted. I wanted to be with a real person. But how could I have been wrong about the aunties? I *couldn't* have imagined it — could I? I managed to say in a quavery voice, "What? There are three mysterious talking dolls at my place and you want to go play some dumb detective game?"

"That must have been some party last night." Rick shook his head. "Let me know when you're back to normal." He started to walk away.

"Rick, wait a minute. This isn't a joke. They really talked to me and —"

"Mark and Scooter like challenges. I'll see if they feel like helping me. See you later."

"Don't you believe me? The aunties *can* talk! If that's the kind of friend you are —"

"Give me a call when you get over it." Rick waved and went out the door.

"Mark and Scooter are morons!" I yelled after him.

I went back to the living room and stood staring at the aunties. I had to admit, they did not look as though they could talk. They looked like three big stuffed dolls propped up on the couch. But I had been so sure they had spoken to me before breakfast — all about manners, and whether they could walk or not . . .

"We do not think much of your choice of friends, Jeremy."

I gasped. "What? What did you say?" The dry, prim, papery voice seemed to come from Mabel.

"Young Richard, or Rick, as you call him, seems to have even fewer manners than you yourself."

"Thanks a whole lot," I said, "for making me look like a total fool in front of my best friend. Rick must think I'm crazy. Why wouldn't you talk when he was here? You made me look like an idiot."

"Antibody indeed!" said a voice that came from Dotty. "How dreadfully vulgar."

"Young people today have no discretion," Mabel said. "No manners and no tact."

"You don't have to tell the whole world about us, you know," said Gladys. At least, the voice came from the fat auntie between the other two, the one Rick had called Auntie Pasto. I was beginning to tell the difference in their voices.

Dotty said, "We are not a freak show, a peep show. We hoped you would be able to keep our secret."

"But why can't you be friends with Rick too?" I asked.

"We do not know him," Mabel replied. "Is he honest and trustworthy and loyal?"

"Of course! He's my friend. At least he *was* my friend . . ."

"For the present, we have no wish to share our secret with anyone else. We trust you will respect our wishes."

So I was the only person the aunties would talk to? But they hardly knew me either.

"So, what do you do for excitement around here, dear boy?" Gladys asked.

"Excitement? Well it's summer holidays. I hang around with my friends, play tennis, watch TV . . ."

"We were thinking of a little outing." Dotty brushed a fuzz from her navy suit. "These old costumes your mother brought home from the theatre are not exactly our style."

"We are in need of summer outfits," Mabel agreed. "These are woollen. The moths will be at us. We would appreciate your assistance, young man."

"Take you shopping? Me? *You*? Sure!" I laughed, picturing myself getting on a bus with the three of them slung over my shoulders. I could just see myself staggering through Eaton's revolving door and up the escalator. I imagined the aunties squashed into a shopping cart as I wheeled them up and down the aisles in the old ladies' section. "Forget it! I've got better things to do." I flicked on a rerun of the Canadian Open tennis championships.

By the end of the week it looked as if the aunties were here to stay. My mother thought them such a charming addition to the house — like pieces of art or furniture — that she just left them on the couch. I was dying to tell someone about them, but after my experience with Rick, who I hadn't heard from since, I knew that the presence of three talking dummies on your living room couch was news you should keep to yourself; I didn't want to be laughed at, or maybe even locked up, for the rest of my life. Whenever I was at the tennis courts, or hanging around the mall, or anywhere near my friends from school, I had to be very careful what I said. Which wasn't easy. Every couple of minutes I'd start saying something like, "The aunties think that . . . " or "Mabel says that . . ." and have to fake a coughing fit or something. It was safer if I didn't open my mouth.

I began spending more and more time with the aunties.

"Tell us about yourself, dear boy," they said.

"Well," I replied, "I'm just kind of a basic, ordinary, average kid. I like tennis and TV and, hmm, there's not much more to tell you."

"Humph." Gladys looked at me as if there was not much there.

I was a bit scared to ask the aunties about themselves. By observing them secretly, I had found out that they never slept — at least, I had never caught them with their eyes closed. And they didn't need to eat or go to the bathroom. They could move their hands and heads a little. What they couldn't do was walk. I offered to teach them, but they seemed quite happy to sit on the couch and do nothing except look out the window at the passing traffic, and talk to me.

"How come you can do everything except walk?" I asked them, wondering if maybe they really could but for some reason did not want me to know.

"It may have something to do with the fact that we have no toes," Mabel said. "Could you walk if your legs ended in stumps?"

I thought for a second or two about offering to stitch toes onto their feet, but then reminded myself I didn't really want them nosing all around the house — or getting outside.

The aunties were completely ignorant about a lot of things. The TV, especially, amazed them. I showed them how to work the remote control, and they watched TV every afternoon when my mother was out of the house. I think they watched the soaps. They were always commenting on the shocking behaviour of the characters. But they loved the slang, and began saying "Dry up" and "Get real," and their favourite, "Get stuffed," which made them wobble against each other with laughter.

I realized too late it was a big mistake to start them on TV. They watched it all the time, like me. But they did nothing but criticize. They were worse than my mother. They would sit there watching a comedy with perfectly straight faces, saying, "Artificial" or "Unrealistic" or "Highly unbelievable." I couldn't watch a thing without them making rude remarks about the silly actors or the weak plots or the ridiculous canned laughter.

The show they especially liked to pick on was one of my favourites, "Real Men/Ideal Men," a game show where a female audience asked male contestants questions like, "Do you open doors for women?" or "What scares you the most?" Every show had a different theme, such as shyness or generosity. Personally, I found it educational.

Why should I care what three old stuffed dolls think? I asked myself. And why had I let a bunch of dumb dolls wreck my friendship with Rick? Well, I'd show them. I decided to call him up for a game of tennis. It felt good dialling his number again.

"Ricketts here."

"Hi, Rick, how about a game of tennis?" I said.

"Jeremy — I've been hoping you'd call! Sure, meet you down at the park in ten minutes."

I was searching an upstairs closet for my tennis

shoes when I came across a little brown book I had never seen before. It was an old album of photographs printed on thin metal squares. I brought it out into the light to see better, and there, in the first picture, were Mabel, Gladys, and Dotty.

Suddenly I felt very cold.

CHAPTER THREE

THE AUNTIES ARE DEMANDING WOMEN

THERE THEY SAT, staring out at me, looking much more like real people than stuffed ones. I took off my glasses, wiped them on my T-shirt, put them back on, and held the old photo closer. It really was the aunties! I rushed downstairs and into the front hall, where my mother was fixing the closet door-knob.

"Who – who are they?" I demanded, holding the picture out to her.

She put down her screwdriver, turned the picture over, and pointed to the names scribbled on the back. "Mabel, Gladys, and Dotty Dermott," she read with a grin.

"But," I cried hoarsely, "they were real people once?"

She smiled again. "I found this old book of tin-types in my favourite antique shop. Only fifty cents. This old photo gave me the idea for the three aunties. And the names on the back were so perfect, I simply had to call them that. I even tried to find clothes like these. What's the matter? You look so strange."

I rushed back upstairs, locked myself in the bathroom, and sat on the john. What a terrifying discovery! I didn't know much about ghosts — especially not how to get them out of your house. I could hide the aunties in a closet so I wouldn't have to look at them — or listen to them. But I imagined them bumping against the door in the night, trying to get out, and figured three ghosts in a closet was worse than three ghosts on the couch. I could give them away — but who'd want them? Or I could sell them — to a costume shop, maybe — although my mother would kill me. Maybe I could throw them in the garbage. That would be easiest. But would they come back to haunt me? Or maybe I could just unstuff them — take them apart limb by limb. Then they would no longer exist! But what if they started to shriek and howl as I began pulling them to pieces? I felt goosebumps on my arms. I knew I could never do it; they were practically my friends. Or had been, until I realized they were real live dead ghosts!

And did my mother have weird magic powers I didn't know about? She *had* been acting kind of suspicious lately, nervous and worried, and usually her mind was somewhere else. Nah, impossible.

Or was it?

I finally reached the conclusion that I would have to face the aunties sometime and tell them what I'd learned. Very slowly, I unlocked the bathroom door and tiptoed downstairs to the living room. It was always kind of cluttered with magazines and books and theatre props my mother was working on. Today there was half a pagoda and three steps that led nowhere, and a vine of plastic grapes. With three stuffed ghosts sitting on the couch watching TV, the room seemed suddenly very eerie. The aunties were watching "Real Men/Ideal Men," with the volume turned low so that my mother, in the kitchen, wouldn't hear.

"Good afternoon," they all said politely, though they seemed annoyed at my interruption.

"My dear, you look as white as a ghost," Dotty said.

"Listen —" I pulled their picture out of my shorts pocket and shoved it in front of them. "Just who are you and what are you doing here and why don't you go back where you came from?"

They were so interested in the photo that for once they did not even comment on my rudeness. They passed it back and forth, exclaiming at the wonderful likeness and the memories it brought back.

"This was taken just before the fire," Gladys told the others. "I remember smelling smoke as we were talking to the photographer."

"What fire?" I asked, my voice catching in my throat. "Don't you see? You're dead! All three of you are dead!"

Mabel looked up at me. "So what?" she said.

"But that means you're — you're ghosts!"

"What did you think we were, talking dolls?" Dotty asked with a giggle.

"I don't want to see you anymore," I said. "Go away. Please."

"What are you scared of?" Gladys asked.

"Yes," Dotty said, "what's changed?"

"Don't you *mind*, being ghosts, being dead? Isn't it scary for you?"

"How do we know *you're* not a ghost?" they said.

"Because I'm real," I said.

"A Real Man? You?" They snickered into their gloves.

"I'm not one of those guys on that show. I mean that I'm alive and you're not, because my mother and I just made you out of stockings and stuff, and just because you used to be real doesn't mean you still are, and — and how did you come back to life anyway?"

Gladys shook her head. "It's a mystery. We have

no idea."

"Did — did my mother have something to do with it?"

"Not that we're aware," Dotty said. "I thought *you* helped make us. Maybe *you* have magical powers, Jeremy." The three of them snickered again.

"Of course I don't." I flopped down on the carpet. Maybe Dotty was right — what had changed? The aunties were the same aunties they had always been.

I looked up at them on the couch. "But what are we going to do?"

"Why do anything?" Mabel asked. "This is a comfortable couch. We are becoming rather interested in the TV, and —" She coughed.

"What Mabel is trying to say," Dotty explained, "is that we've become rather fond of you, Jeremy."

"You're not bad company — for a real person," Gladys said, trying to wink.

I felt myself getting red. It was their first compliment. "Oh, get stuffed," I joked, and we all had a good laugh.

"About that shopping trip —" Dotty began.

"Dream on," I said. "I'm not taking you anywhere."

The only person I could tell about the aunties having once been real people was Rick. I was sure he would want to know about the old photo I'd found. I went up to my mother's bedroom and dialled his number.

"Ricketts here," he answered on the first ring.

"Rick!" I said. "It's me. Look, I know you didn't believe me about the three aunties, but it's all true, and now things have gotten even stranger. It turns out the aunties were —"

"I waited for you at the tennis courts for an hour," Rick interrupted. "Where were you? Home playing with your aunties?"

"Oh, gee, sorry. I forgot all about our game. But I just made a discovery. The aunties are even more mysterious than I thought. I could use some help to —"

"No kidding you need help. But all the help you need is right in your own home. Feeling nervous? Feeling sick? What you need is an Auntie Histamine. And an Auntie Septic Auntie Biotic! Ha ha ha ha ha ha ha!"

"Ha, ha," I snarled. "I hope you know you have a radically sick sense of humour! Just for that I'm not going to tell you a thing!" I slammed down the phone and slumped down on the bed. Rick had probably been saving that joke up for a while. He'd probably been sitting by the phone just hoping I'd call. Some friend! Why had I called him, anyway?

Maybe I was getting too hyper. After all, finding the photo hadn't really changed anything. I went down to the living room.

"What were you saying about a shopping trip?" I asked.

Dotty smiled. "So glad you remembered. You will take us shopping, won't you, Jeremy dear."

"But what's wrong with what you've got on? You look fine to me."

"My dear boy," said Mabel, "it is neither good manners nor good hygiene to wear the same garments day and night, week in and week out. We require a change of clothing each. We simply must go shopping."

"You want different clothes, I'll lend you a pair of shorts. My parrot and watermelon ones are getting kind of tight. Or my old grey sweatsuit, or my mom's neon leotard."

The aunties gazed off into the distance.

"Look, I've got exactly nine dollars and eighty-two cents," I explained. The lawn-mowing business I was trying to get going was not exactly booming.

"A fortune!" Dotty breathed.

"This is not the dark ages. Nine eighty-two wouldn't even buy you new gloves. Anyway, if I had any money, I'd buy a new bike. I wouldn't waste my cash on doll clothes! Get real!"

"Wealth is no excuse for sarcasm," Mabel said firmly. She put a glove to her mouth as if she was about to tell me a secret. "We could not help but overhear a telephone conversation of your mother's this morning. We are aware that she is having some difficulty just now making ends meet. We know that the theatre where she works is having financial troubles. We therefore appeal to you, Jeremy, as a gentleman of means, to help us in our time of need."

I did not see why I should spend my cash on three old ghosts. Just because they could talk didn't mean they could talk me out of my money.

"Think of it as an adventure," Gladys said encouragingly. "We're just dying to get out . . ."

"Oh, please," Dotty begged. "We needn't go far. A small shop would do. We do not wish to make a spectacle of ourselves, you know."

"Well," I said slowly, "I think there's an old dress shop downtown. I guess we could *try* it. But remember, I've got less than ten bucks. And my broken-down old bike can only carry one of you. Who's it going to be?" I said there was no way I was taking Gladys, who was so overweight she'd probably flatten the bike tires.

Mabel insisted that, as the eldest, she should go. Finally all three agreed that Dotty should go, since she had the best fashion sense. Mabel took a sheet of yellow notepaper and a fountain pen from her purse and made a list of their sizes, grumbling all the while about the clumsiness of her gloves and what fine penmanship she had once had.

As soon as my mother left the house, I hoisted Dotty over my shoulder and carried her outside. I stuffed her into my bike carrier. Her legs dangled on either side of the front wheel. I propped up her head by leaning forward and resting my chin against her hat. Off we set, splashing through puddles and bouncing over bumps. Dotty had never been on a bike before, and she was so excited she could hardly stay on.

"Not so fast — I've got a stitch in my side," she joked as we bumped over the railroad tracks, and we both laughed like crazy.

"My, how the city has changed!" she exclaimed. "I hardly recognize a thing."

I veered to avoid a bus. "What? You mean you used to live right here — in this city?"

"Yes. What is so odd about that? I had a charming little house on Duke Street, and my cousins lived just around the corner on Scott." She laughed. "Did you think ghosts came from strange and faraway places?"

Well, yes, that's what I *had* thought. Out of curiosity, I biked a few blocks out of our way, to the corner of Scott and Duke. A solid wall of department stores and office buildings took up the entire block.

Dotty sighed. "There used to be a little row of crabapple trees there, at the front gate. And where that bus stop is, I used to slip through the hedge by the pump whenever I wanted to run over and see Mabel and Gladys. Well, never mind. It was a long time ago. Let's shop!"

I shivered when Dotty talked about the crabapple trees and pump as if they were real. It made me feel, somehow, as if I wasn't.

I kept to the back alleys as much as I could so no one — especially Rick — would spot me riding around town with a doll in my carrier. We reached the main street without attracting any attention. Across from us was a small store with a large sign above the door:

ROSE'S CLOTHES:
Quality Antique and Second-Hand Apparel
(Ritzy Rags with Low Price Tags)

I did some fancy wheelwork across the street. Just as we bounced over the curb in front of the bank next to Rose's, disaster struck. A big red-haired policeman appeared out of nowhere. He took one look and flagged me down.

I got off my bike and wheeled it towards him, shielding Dotty from his view as best I could.

CHAPTER FOUR
THE OLD CLOTHES CAPER

"RIDING DOUBLE IS ILLEGAL," the policeman said sternly. "So is speeding, jay-crossing, failing to signal, and riding on a vehicle that should be in the dump. Your friend there can step down."

"No, she can't," I said. "She, I, um . . . I was just taking her into that store by the bank." I pointed to Rose's Clothes.

"You *will* get off that bike!" The cop glared down at Dotty. Then he frowned, blushed, and cleared his throat. "I knew she wasn't real, kid," he mumbled. "Just joking, eh? Get that bike fixed or next time I'll take it off the street, you hear?" He hurried away, glancing sneakily around to make sure no one had heard him talking to a doll.

"He thought I was real!" Dotty hooted. "Did you hear him ordering me around? Dear me," she said with a giggle, "I was so tempted to tell him to stuff it."

I carried Dotty into Rose's. It was a dimly lit shop with large front windows displaying old hats and jewellery. Racks of dresses, gowns, and coats filled the entire floorspace so that there was barely room to move. Dotty could not resist a small gasp of pleasure.

"Shh," I warned, as a woman hung up the phone and came towards us.

"Hi, I'm Rose," she said. "Ah, I see you've brought a mannequin! She'd be *perfect* in the front window modelling hats, and yes — the yellow tea dress that just came in. How much do you want for her?"

Dotty shuddered and went limp in my arms.

"She's not for sale," I said firmly. "I'm just here to shop."

"She's such a doll I can see why you want to keep her." The store owner smiled. "But let's make a deal. How about I rent her from you for a week? She'll help sales, and I'll pay you — twenty dollars?"

"Twenty doll —?" I gasped. "For sitting in the window?" Great! The aunties could earn their own clothes allowance instead of using up *my* money. "It's a deal!" I said. "Her name is Dotty."

"This must be my lucky week," Rose said. "Last month I nearly closed, business was so bad. But then three fellows bought this building — they want to remodel the basement or something — and they've let me stay on in the shop for only half the rent. Things are really looking up."

Things were looking up for me too. Twenty easy

bucks! I signed the receipt for Dotty and dashed out to my bike without a backward glance.

"You rented our cousin out for common hire?" Mabel exclaimed.

"Sold into bondage in a rag and bone shop?" Gladys cried weakly.

"But think of the money," I told them. "Twenty bucks just for spending a week in a window. A nice change of view — you could all take your turn. Besides," I added, quoting my mother, "you appreciate the value of money and spend it more wisely when you earn it yourself."

"A week!" Gladys moaned. "Oh, what will become of our poor Dotty?"

"We miss her already. I did not know you were so heartless," Mabel said.

Me, heartless? I felt like saying. I happened to be the only person in the room who had any heart at all. It was too soft, that was the problem. I always ended up giving in to the aunties. To set their minds at rest, I promised I would check up on Dotty every day.

Two days later I remembered my promise. I cruised past Rose's on my way home from the tennis courts.

Dotty sat stiffly on an antique chair in the display

window, wearing a fancy yellow gown and a dazed expression. When she caught sight of me her eyes seemed to light up. Her gloves shook as she motioned for me to come into the shop.

I grinned encouragingly and held up four fingers, to show her that in only four more days she would be back home again. "Think of the money!" I mouthed, and waved good-bye.

A passing policeman glared at me suspiciously. It was the same red-haired cop who had stopped me in front of the bank for riding double. He probably thought I was slightly insane, waving at my reflection in a store window. I zipped away before he could grab me or my bike.

When I got home my mother met me at the door.

"Dreadful news, Jeremy," she announced in a dramatic whisper. "Dotty is missing!"

"Uh, it's okay," I mumbled. "I know where she is. I, uh, took her out."

My mother raised her eyebrows. "Aren't you rather young to be taking out older women?"

I shrugged and nodded. It was getting difficult to talk to my mother. We definitely weren't as comfortable with each other as we'd been before. I had a feeling she was getting suspicious about all the time I spent alone with the aunties. I was suspicious of her too. I couldn't stop wondering if she had had something to do with bringing the aunties to life. I didn't really think so, but what else could explain it?

I headed for the living room and flicked on the TV so I could talk to Mabel and Gladys. Before I could tell them anything, we heard Mom's footsteps approaching, and I picked up a magazine to pretend I'd gone in there to read. It was a fashion magazine. I quickly put it down.

"I suppose you took Dotty over to Rick's or something," my mother said, pausing in the living room doorway. "Don't forget to bring her back." She looked around. "You know, the living room does seem more spacious with only two of them. Maybe we should get rid of all three aunties. Maybe we could even sell them, make a few bucks."

"Sell the aunties?" I exclaimed. "Sell them? Never!"

"Think of the money, though. You could get the new bike you want."

"No way. They're not for sale. If they go, I go. You can't —"

"All right, all right, Jeremy, calm yourself. I suppose I'd miss the old things myself. If they really mean more than a new bike to you, keep them, by all means." She came over and ruffled my hair. "And by the way, I think you've been watching far too much

TV lately. It seems to be on all the time. It isn't healthy, mentally or physically. It's a bad influence on you. You've become so withdrawn lately. Maybe we should get rid of the TV. *That* would make more room in here."

She went out. I heaved a sigh of relief and turned to the aunties. I expected they'd be grateful that I had just saved them from disappearing out of my life, but they looked quite upset.

"No need to get nervous," I told them. "I'd never let her sell you."

"Of *course* not!" Gladys said. "Why sell us when you can make money *renting* us out to clothing stores?"

I remembered that I had come home with news for the aunties.

"About time!" they sniffed, after I told them I'd seen Dotty. "So, how is she?"

"Well," I said, "well, as a matter of fact, she doesn't look exactly thrilled about being there, but . . ."

"You mean you did not even talk to her?" Mabel cried. "Young man, Gladys and I are worried to death. Dotty has never been alone like this before. She will be frightened and homesick. This brainless scheme cannot go on any longer. We insist you bring her straight back home."

"Impossible. The store's closed by now, and besides, I signed a contract for a week. You want new clothes, don't you?"

"Jeremy! No amount of money is worth such suffering. We must see Dotty at once. If you cannot bring her back to us, we must go to her. Without delay."

I imagined myself careening through the city with two aunties strapped to my wobbly fenders. "My bike will never take it."

"We have already discussed the seating arrangements," Mabel said. "Gladys can have the carrier, and I shall ride shotgun, as they say on TV, on your, er, rat-trap. We can slip out after midnight when the streets are empty. We simply must satisfy ourselves that dear Dotty is all right."

"What danger," I said, "can a stuffed doll possibly come to in an old clothes store? And anyway, why do you think you can tell me what to do? You're not my real aunties, you know. I don't have to listen to you."

Gladys looked furious. I stayed out of reach of her umbrella.

"Then if anything happens to Dotty it will be your responsibility," Mabel said coldly. "After all, *you* took her there in the first place."

"Right, I never should have let you talk me into

that dumb shopping trip. Okay, then, we'll go. You can see for yourselves that Dotty is perfectly fine."

My alarm woke me at one a.m. I looked out my window. The street was strangely quiet and empty. I slipped downstairs and found Mabel and Gladys perched on the edge of the couch clutching their purses. They were also armed: Mabel with her wooden cane and Gladys with her flowery umbrella. I wasn't sure what they were expecting.

I carried them outside and strapped them carefully onto my bike. Normally I didn't go biking around the city in the middle of the night — my mom would have had a panic attack. But somehow, with two aunties along, I didn't feel scared at all. It was even kind of exciting. And this time I didn't have to worry about anyone seeing me as we rode clumsily through the silent city to Rose's Clothes.

Dotty looked like a ghost in the pale glow from the streetlights. Her eyes were dull and hopeless. When she saw us she started forward in her chair. "Help!" we heard faintly through the glass. "Help me."

"She's going to faint!" Gladys said.

"I knew she was in trouble," Mabel said. "I knew it! Wheel us to the door, Jeremy."

"Don't be ridiculous," I said, pedalling up to the

door. "We can't break in!"

"It's an old door." Gladys leaned out of the carrier to examine the lock. "Can you pass me a hairpin, please, Mabel?"

I watched open-mouthed as Gladys grasped the hairpin in her soft gloved hand, inserted it expertly into the keyhole, gave a quick twist and a pull, and pushed the door open. "Bingo," she said.

"How did you do that?"

"I watch far too much TV," she replied.

"What are we waiting for?" Mabel asked. "Park the bicycle and take us inside."

"It's illegal," I protested. "We'll get ourselves in trouble."

"Oh, don't be so stuffy," Gladys said.

I parked the bike around the corner and carried them inside, closing the door behind me.

CHAPTER FIVE

THREE MEN AND A DUMMY

IN THE DIM GLOW from the streetlight, the racks of dresses looked like limp headless women lurking in the shadows.

Mabel and Gladys leaned forward in my arms. "Dotty?" they whispered. "Dotty, we're here."

I made my way to the window. Dotty collapsed into our arms with a sob. We fell to the floor in a muddle of arms and legs and explanations.

"I'm so glad you've come!" Dotty cried. "Please, please take me home. I've tried to be brave and do my duty, but I never wanted to stay, and now I'm afraid those men will harm me with their hammers and pickaxes and —"

"She's been dreaming, poor dear." Gladys gave her a squeeze.

"Her imagination has run away with her, here all alone in the dark," Mabel said.

"No," Dotty cried. "There are men. They come in every night . . ."

When we had calmed Dotty down we sat on the floor and listened to her story. Each night after midnight, she said, three men let themselves into the store through the front door. They carried picks and shovels and other tools down to the basement. All night, hammering and muffled thudding from below shook Dotty's chair. Then at dawn the men would leave, as quietly as they had come. "At first I thought they were ghosts," Dotty told us. "I was sure the store was haunted. But on the second night they caught sight of me sitting here. They must have thought I was real!" She giggled nervously. "I suppose I gave them a scare. One came over, his hammer raised as if he was going to beat the stuffing right out of me. Then he said, 'It's just a window dummy, boys,' and they left me alone."

"Foul intruders!" Gladys cried. "Vicious burglars! Poor dear Dotty, how did you survive? We're here to rescue you at last."

"Ghosts? Burglars?" I laughed. "Don't you remember? Rose, the shop lady, said three new owners were remodelling the basement. Cheer up, Dotty. It's nothing to worry about. Now let's clear out of here and get back home."

"Don't be a bonehead!" Gladys said. "If the three men are the owners, why do they sneak in at night to do their work? They're crooks, all right."

"If they're crooks," I said, "what are they doing down there with hammers and things?"

"Digging, of course," Gladys replied. "For

buried treasure. Have you no imagination?"

"What did they look like?" I asked Dotty. "Crooks or remodellers?"

"They wore hats, and had their collars turned up. I couldn't see them clearly in the dark."

I suddenly remembered something. "D-do you remember that W-wanted Poster Rick was talking about that day he came over?" I couldn't keep my teeth from chattering.

At that moment we heard a key in the front door and someone cursing. The door swung open and three dark shadows crept stealthily into the shop.

"The door wasn't even locked," a voice growled. "That Old Clothes Rose is a pretty careless dame. I'm glad this business will be finished tonight. We'll grab the loot and no one the wiser." Their footsteps creaked across the floor towards the basement stairs. In a few minutes we heard the dull sound of hammering.

I crawled shakily from beneath a rack of dresses and rejoined the aunties. "W-w-what are we going to do?" I stammered. "Let's g-get out of here before they come up and find us. Quick!"

"Why, Jeremy," Gladys whispered, "I didn't know you were so lily-livered. There are three burglars in the basement and all you can think of is to turn tail and run. Have you no backbone? What a spineless young man you are."

I was glad she couldn't see my face go red. "As a matter of fact," I said, "I happen to be the only person here with any backbone at all. I don't know about the rest of you, but I'm leaving. We could all be killed!" I stood up. The floor creaked ominously. I caught my breath and sat right back down again, close to the aunties.

"I told you he's weak-kneed," Gladys said. "I thought you would be eager to face danger in defence of three female companions. Where's your guts? Where's your courage? Where's your sense of chivalry, boy?"

"It's fine for you three to pretend to be brave," I replied in a trembling whisper. "If those men come up and find us, who do you think they'll go after? Me, that's who! They can't hurt you. *You're* not alive. If they whacked you with a hammer, you'd bounce right back. If they pumped you full of bullets, you'd probably be fine after a few stitches. I'm the only one here with a *right* to be afraid. They could *kill* me. I'm getting out of here."

"It is quite natural to be frightened in a situation such as this," Mabel told me kindly. "You would hardly be a normal boy if you were not. Dotty is frightened too, and Gladys is only talking like that to give herself courage. Even I am not fully at ease.

But what we must all do is remain calm and decide upon the best course of action."

"I say we leave right now," I said.

"Don't you want to catch the crooks?" Gladys asked impatiently.

"Sure," I lied, "but we've got to be realistic. Those guys will hear our footsteps if we try to call the cops. The phone's right there — next to the basement stairs. And if we try to lock them down there, they'll break through in no time with those pickaxes. And if we do phone the cops, we'll have to explain what *we're* doing here in the middle of the night. They'll arrest us for breaking in, and book us as accomplices. And if we *do* escape," I said, "we'll have to either leave Dotty behind or explain her absence to Rose tomorrow."

"Of course we must take Dotty," Mabel said firmly. "We cannot leave her here."

"But if we take Dotty," I said, "Rose will report her missing in the morning and I'll be the prime suspect in a break-and-enter."

We couldn't even stay put and do nothing — I didn't like the idea of being discovered there in the morning by Rose, along with two extra mannequins, shivering (or dead!) on the floor. The aunties were right. We had to do *something*.

At last we agreed on a plan. That is, the aunties

agreed. I still wanted to hop on my bike and burn rubber all the way home, with or without the aunties. But since I didn't enjoy being called a spineless, gutless, weak-kneed, lily-livered coward, I said, "Sure, great plan, let's go for it."

Their plan combined all the ideas we had discussed, and it meant waiting until almost dawn. Mabel would be posted at the telephone ready to dial 911, the emergency code. (She said she thought it would be interesting speaking to someone other than me for a change.) And Gladys, who in her days as a live person had sung alto in the church choir, and even tenor when they were short of men, would be propped by the locked basement door. If the three men tried to force their way through before help arrived, she would shout in her deepest voice: "Drop your weapons! You're surrounded! Step through that door and I'll blow your gizzards to Shanghai!" Dotty would stay in the window as a lookout while I ran for help.

We waited nervously, listening to the sound of hammering from below. The hours crept by. While we waited, the aunties told me a bit more about their past. They hardly ever talked about themselves, but I think they were desperate to keep me from leaving. I found out that none of them had ever been married; they had continued to live in their family homes even after their parents had died. None of them had ever had a job — they seemed surprised when I asked.

"In our day," Mabel explained, "it was not considered proper for ladies to work. We had to make do with the small income our fathers left us."

"Although," said Gladys, "we were not without talent."

"And could have used the extra money," Dotty added.

"If we were living now," Gladys said, "you can bet we'd start up our own business and be rolling in the dough."

They also told me about their hobbies: Mabel had enjoyed sewing, and gardening before her leg gave out on her; Gladys, besides singing, liked reading mysteries and spy novels, and Dotty liked shopping and going to the theatre with her gentlemen friends.

Their conversation didn't make me feel any less nervous. In fact, I felt more jittery than ever. It was like listening to ghost stories in the dark. Literally. The more real the aunties seemed, having a past, and hobbies, and everything, the less real *I* felt. I couldn't believe I was actually sitting there on the floor of a downtown clothing store in the middle of the night with three burglars bumping around below! Things like that just didn't happen to me.

To take my mind off our wait, the aunties asked me what I planned to be when I grew up. I didn't really know. I thought over all the things I used to want to be, like a cop, a professional tennis player, a computer whiz. At the moment all I wanted to be was normal, which meant home safe in bed.

"*My* fondest dream," Mabel murmured, "was to have a child."

"What?" Mabel seemed much too old to have a child, and besides, what kind of baby would she have? I pictured a little wrinkled rag doll.

"I do not mean an infant!" she whispered sternly. "I was never married, my dear boy! No, my dream was to have a child, perhaps a nephew, whom I could guide and influence, whom I could raise up to be a good and responsible citizen." She coughed. "I suppose one could say that my dream has come true . . ."

"What do you mean?" I asked.

"She means *you*, Jeremy," Gladys said. "Can't you take a hint?"

"Me?" It was strange to think that Mabel thought of me as a nephew. But on the other hand, I thought of her as an auntie.

"It must be nearly dawn," Dotty whispered. The sky outside the window did seem a little lighter.

"Look alive, Jeremy! Get us into position."

I picked up Gladys, who was ready with the hairpin, and staggered quietly across the floor. I couldn't help admiring her bravery. I didn't want to be anywhere near the basement door.

In the dark I bumped into a rack of hats — it tilted and fell. I held my breath, waiting for the crash. But Gladys threw herself to the floor, and cushioned the rack with her large soft belly. The only sound was a stifled cry from me.

"Dry up," she hissed. "Don't ruin the plan now! Pick me up."

I tiptoed in terror to the basement door and propped her beside it. Inch by inch, I pulled the door closed. Without waiting to watch her lock it, I silently made my way back for Mabel. The floor creaked loudly. It's never going to work, I thought, as I placed Mabel by the phone with trembling hands. I handed her Dotty's cigarette holder to help her dial, and I crept back to the window to wait. My one ambition was to get out of that store alive.

"Jeremy!" Dotty hissed. "The hammering has stopped! Run for it!"

I thought I could still hear hammering, but I realized it was the pounding of my heart. Not worrying about the sound of my footsteps, I raced to the front door and into the street.

At last I was safe! I drew in big gulps of air. All I had to do now was complete my part of the plan: run for help, then go back to the store and rescue the aunties. Or, I thought suddenly, I could simply head for home and leave the aunties to save themselves — since they were so brave. I ran towards my bike.

A police cruiser nosed out of an alley in the next block. The officer at the wheel caught sight of me. There was no choice now but to continue with the aunties' plan. Trembling, I raced towards the car, waving my arms wildly. A tall, red-haired policeman stopped the car and climbed out.

CHAPTER SIX

THE REWARDS OF BRAVERY

"YOU AGAIN!" the policeman said. "I'm beginning to wonder about you."

"Please, I'm not a lunatic," I stammered. "Really. Quick, you've got to come — there's a break-and-enter going on up the street and —"

"How about *you* come with *me* ?" he said. "Get in the other side."

I got into the cruiser, afraid he would drive me to the station for questioning, or throw me into a padded cell without bothering with questions. "I was just out for a morning bike ride," I babbled as he began to drive, "and as I went past Rose's Clothes I happened to notice that the door was open and there were weird noises of hammering coming from inside, so I raced to find a cop, I mean policeman —"

I stopped talking when he picked up his radio and said the street name and some numbers. He stopped in front of the bank beside Rose's. Another cruiser pulled up beside us. "Wait right here," he ordered. "If there's any shooting, get down on the floor." He and the other officers disappeared.

But there was no time to wait around. Now that

the police were there I *had* to get the aunties out of the store. They were proof that I'd been inside.

I was terrified of going back in there. Now the robbers — *or* the cops — might get me. My hands shook and my legs were like Jell-O. Maybe because I felt as limp and weak as an auntie, I realized suddenly how helpless they must feel without me. I raced into the store.

"All clear," they whispered, poking their heads out from behind racks of clothing.

I scooped up Gladys from her spot near the splintered basement door, carried her outside to my bike, and stuffed her into the carrier. Then I ran back for Dotty and Mabel. I got Mabel on the rat-trap and somehow tied Dotty to the handlebars with her yellow belt. The three of them told me, between gasps as we wobbled full-speed towards home, how the police had burst into the store, broken the lock on the basement door, and raced down the steps without even noticing the three of them. They had heard nothing from the basement before I came back to rescue them. Our plan seemed to have worked!

I pulled into the driveway. Suddenly there was a loud BANG! followed by another BANG!

"Duck!" I yelled. "We've been followed! They're shooting!"

"What are you, wool-for-brains?" Gladys said. "Those were your bike tires exploding."

I looked away so they wouldn't see me blush. "I knew that," I mumbled. "I was just kidding you."

I carried the aunties into the living room and set them on the couch. I grabbed a ginger ale and a pickled beet from the fridge and scooted up to my room. My mother was softly snoring across the hall. With a huge sigh of relief I flopped onto my bed without bothering to undress and instantly fell asleep.

When I woke up I reached over sleepily to shut off the alarm, but realized after a second or two that it wasn't buzzing. I peered at the orange numbers — 4:12 p.m. Sun was pouring in the window. I looked outside and noticed a strange car parked in the drive. At first I thought I was still dreaming. Then I remembered what had happened during the night: not a dream, a nightmare! Maybe it was an unmarked police car in the drive. By getting out of the cop's car to rescue the aunties in the store, I had escaped police custody! Now they had tracked me down. I thought of running away, but I wouldn't get very far on a bike with two flat tires, or on my shaking, weak-kneed, lily-livered legs. I figured I might as well give myself up. I had heard jail wasn't really that bad: TV, lots of food, no schoolwork . . .

I straightenend my rumpled sweatshirt, put on my glasses, and went slowly downstairs to the kitchen. Rose was having a coffee with my mother.

"Here's the boy you're looking for," my mother said.

"Well, congratulations," Rose said. "I hear you helped capture three bank robbers this morning. They tunnelled into the bank through the basement of my store. The police were there when I went to open up this morning and told me all about it. They asked me for your address. I suppose they want it so they can give you the reward."

"Reward? For me? Wow! How much?"

"Oh, plenty, I'm sure," Rose said. "At least a thousand, I would think. Maybe more."

"Wow! That's great!" I could get a new bike! I could get two new bikes! I couldn't wait to tell Rick how I had captured the robbers all by myself!

"The funny thing is," Rose said as she got up to leave, "the robbers seem to have stolen your mannequin, Dotty. That's why I came. I'm so terribly sorry, Jeremy. She's the only thing they took from the store — I can't understand it. Would you accept a hundred dollars towards replacing her? I know it's not much, but . . ." She passed me two crisp red bills.

It was tempting, but of course I couldn't take it,

since Dotty was sitting safe and sound in the next room.

My mother looked at me strangely.

"Well," she said, when Rose had left, "this is all most peculiar, Jeremy. Correct me if I've got it wrong, but I understand you were out for a pre-dawn bike ride and just happened to foil a bank robbery? And another funny thing: Dotty has mysteriously reappeared on the couch — wearing a quite horrid mustard-coloured outfit. You had her out at a second-hand store? Just what's going on, son?"

I bit my lips. I couldn't give the aunties' secret away.

"We've got to talk, Jeremy. You're acting so suspicious lately."

"I'm not suspicious of you," I said. I crossed my fingers behind my back.

"Of course I don't mean suspicious of *me*. I mean you're not yourself these last few weeks. You've been acting very strange. Come, sit down and tell me what's bothering you."

"I can explain everything," I said, ducking past her, "later." I sped up the stairs.

I sat on my bed, thinking about the reward I would get, wondering how I should spend it. Maybe on a Nintendo or a mini-computer or my own personal phone. I could be just like Rick. I'd be rich!

Thanks to the aunties. I knew I owed the adventure to them. Wait till I told Rick I had got the reward without even trying! So much for feeding information into his computer. I had the aunties. Who needed all his fancy equipment? I went into my mother's room to phone him up. After hearing about my amazing night, and the reward, he'd have to believe what I'd told him about the aunties!

"Ricketts here," came the familiar answer.

"Hey, Rick! Jeremy. Guess what! Last night I had this incredibly wild adventure with the aunties chasing these bank robbers, and we caught them, and the cops are going to give me a humungous reward! Look, you've got to come over and apologize to the aunties for calling them names. I'm sure they'd talk to you if you only —"

" . . . or leave your name and number after the beep," said Rick's voice on the answering machine. I muttered a bad word under my breath.

"Except," the recording went on, "if you happen to be a certain Auntie Social type, you don't have to leave your number, because I know it, and I'd really rather hear you apologize for your Auntie Social attitude in person than on my answering machine. That is, if you aren't too busy socializing with your precious Aunties. *Beeeeeeeeep.*"

I repeated the bad word into the receiver and

hung up. *Me*, apologize? He must be joking. *I* hadn't done anything wrong. Other than try to introduce him to the aunties, who he refused to believe were real. He had no imagination, that was Rick's problem!

Downstairs, I told the aunties about Rick's rude message. "It's all over between him and me. We'll never be friends again."

"Real friendships cannot be broken or mended by talking though a telephone machine box," Mabel said. "Your notions of friendship seem to have come from television."

"Flimsy and shallow," Gladys added.

"As if you three would know anything about real friendship," I muttered.

My mother came in and turned on the local evening news.

"The infamous Banks Brothers, notorious criminals and escape artists, were apprehended early this morning by our own regional police force as they attempted another bank robbery right here in the city!" We watched as three old men in trench coats and gangster-style hats were led into cruisers by police officers.

"Edward, Harvey, and Mortimer Banks, well known in Canada for their long career of criminal activities, were caught in the act after tunnelling into the bank basement from a neighbouring store. A woman of undetermined age, seated in a bicycle carrier . . ." The newscaster peered at his notes. "Er, yes, seated in a bicycle carrier . . . was spotted near the crime scene by an early morning dog-walker, but no evidence was found by police to support the theory of accomplices.

The Brothers were captured after an observant youngster tipped off police."

"My Jeremy!" my mother said proudly.

I blushed, and grinned. A commercial came on.

My mother went out to the kitchen to start supper, saying, "You're a genuine hero, Jeremy, old trout!"

I realized I'd forgotten to tell the aunties about the reward.

"I forgot to mention," I said, trying not to look in their eyes, "Rose, the Old Clothes lady, said the police are going to give me a reward. I, um, suppose it should really go to you three. If it had been up to me, the Banks Brothers would have gotten away with the robbery. You were the brave ones. You should get the reward."

Gladys slapped a pudgy knee and tried to stifle her laughter. "If your schoolmates could see you now! Trying to give up your reward money to three stuffed dolls!"

"But I was a real coward." I looked at the floor. "You were the ones who made the plan work. I-I almost ran off and left you there alone."

"But you *didn't* run off, did you!" Dotty smiled.

"Bravery is only fear turned inside out," Mabel added. "Like a piece of old clothing. Ahem. You earned the reward, Jeremy."

"And we take back those jokes about your body," Dotty said. "You are neither brainless nor gutless. You were pretty brave — for a real person."

"Well," I said, "when you put it like that . . ." For once it felt good to give in to the aunties.

"Shh," Dotty said. "The news is back on."

"This news bulletin just in," continued the announcer. "The Banks Brothers have escaped police custody and are once again at large. Police sources admit that the Brothers escaped less than an hour after they had been taken to police headquarters. Shortly afterward, the same bank at which they were caught was robbed of a large amount of cash. Unsubstantiated reports say the Brothers made their escape on a stolen motorcycle and were pursued by two constables, who followed them as they headed west out of the city. The constables lost the Brothers' trail after their motorcycle left the road near a bridge. The money has not been recovered. The Brothers are believed armed and dangerous."

"Good gracious!" Mabel exclaimed. "This is dreadful news! How dare those men escape after we went to all the trouble of capturing them?"

"The audacity!" Gladys said. "The nerve of them! But what else is to be expected from three crooks?"

"I wish the TV news man had given more information about the Brother's escape," Dotty said. "We have so little to go on."

"Hey, wait a minute," I said. "It's not our fault the Banks Brothers escaped from jail. It's not our problem. I'm not getting mixed up with those guys again."

"I have never in my life met such a dull boy," Gladys said with a sigh. "What is the world coming to?"

"Those guys are probably out of the province by now," I told them, "and you couldn't catch them even if I helped you, which I have no intention of doing. So sit back and relax. Let the cops do their job."

Then a terrible thought occurred to me. "Hey — since the Banks Brothers escaped again, does that mean we won't get a reward after all?"

"Don't be silly. We'll get one," Gladys said. "Of course we will."

Gladys sounded so sure I cheered up, and I went

out to the kitchen for supper. I knew exactly how I would spend some of the reward money. I had to get my mother to help, since I had no idea what sort of outfits the aunties would like.

"You want to spend your reward money on clothes for the aunties?" she said, raising her eyebrows. "I really do not understand the way your mind works, Jeremy." But she agreed to go shopping at Rose's and see what she could find. "I've got time tomorrow morning before work," she said. "You can pay me back when you get your reward cheque."

That night I dreamt about being rich.

CHAPTER SEVEN

THE GREAT FISHING
EXPEDITION

WHEN I CAME DOWNSTAIRS the next morning, my mother had already left for work. The aunties were watching "Real Men/Ideal Men." The game show host came on the screen, smiling and joking.

"On our last program," he announced, "our panel of judges decided that Real Men Don't Hold Grudges! And the key word was FRRRIENDSHIP! On today's show we'll find out if it's true that Real Men Don't Wimp Out. And the key word for today is — BRRRAVERY!"

"Such an absurd show," Dotty said. "What would that silly host know about bravery?"

"Humph," said Mabel. "We thought this generation was beyond nonsense about men and bravery. There is a fine line between bravery and foolishness."

"Let's meet our guest contestants," cried the announcer, "to discover if they are in fact REAL MEN!"

"Is he joking?" Gladys scoffed. "How would

anyone ever believe those fellows are real men? They're only three inches high!"

"It's the camera angle!" I said. "If it's such an absurd show, why watch it?"

"We're waiting for the *news*," Dotty whispered. "There might be more on about those Banks Brothers."

"You know, Jeremy, we were talking last night about the television set," Mabel said. "We hope you will not be on television when you are presented with the reward. Suppose they shrank you down to fit inside the TV and you were not able to get back out again. We would miss you."

I looked at the aunties. It was hard to tell when they were joking.

Over a bowl of Swheatios and some warmed-up lasagne, I decided it might be a good idea to phone the police station to see if I should come in and pick up the cheque in person. I looked up the number and explained who I was to the receptionist.

"I'm sorry," she told me, "your name doesn't appear in our file on the Banks Brothers. No reward cheque has been issued. They have not been arrested yet, you know. Until they are, I'm afraid there is no reward."

Slowly I hung up the phone. I didn't feel like finishing my lasagne. I couldn't even make myself tell the aunties the bad news. I wanted to go for a bike ride. That's when I remembered my tires had blown.

I wheeled my bike downtown. No reward. No cheque. No money. No new bike. I went to my bank and took out thirty-five bucks, hoping it would be enough to buy new tires. Then I took out the thirty-nine dollars and twenty-two cents that were left, totally emptying my savings account. With the Banks Brothers on the loose again, I figured the bank wasn't the safest place to leave my money.

I found a pair of used heavy-duty tires for only $23.95. Cruising home, I passed a hardware store with a piggybank in the window. It was in the shape of a pink cadillac. It made me think of my mom. All year she had been driving a beat-up second-hand convertible whose roof was permanently stuck halfway down. Without my reward money of course I couldn't afford to buy her a real car, but I went into the store and bought her the piggybank. It only cost five bucks. I knew she'd love it.

I got home around lunchtime and deposited what was left of my money safely inside one of the couch cushions where the aunties sat. They agreed it would be safer with them than in a bank.

They didn't seem to notice that I was not exactly cheerful.

"How do you like our summer costumes, Jeremy?" Dotty asked.

I realized they were in different clothes.

"Your dear mother came in this morning with complete new outfits for all of us. We thought it was wonderfully sweet and thoughtful and generous of her. Well, what do you think?"

I thought I should point out that the new outfits were *my* idea, and that the reason my mother had got them was because I knew the aunties would never have allowed me to dress them. But I didn't.

Dotty was wearing an old-fashioned black bathing costume complete with gloves and striped stockings. Gladys's dress was white and billowy, her hat covered with ribbons. Mabel wore a sailor suit and navy straw hat. They looked weird.

"We adore them, don't we, girls?" Dotty said. "Your mother is so kind!"

I supposed it had never occurred to the aunties that I could be kind and generous and thoughtful — not to mention tactful.

"They are just the thing for a fishing trip," Mabel said. "Do you happen to have a rowboat, Jeremy?"

"We've decided to go fishing," Gladys explained. "And we know just the place. It's the loveliest spot, all peaceful and shady. You'll like it."

"I don't know what you three think you're up to," I said, "but you can forget it. I'm not taking you anywhere. I hate fish, and I don't own a boat."

"But you have money now. You can buy one," Dotty suggested happily.

"I don't have money," I said, and explained what I had found out.

"Oh, well," Gladys said, "cheer up. Too much money is not good for you anyway."

"Right," I said. "Sure. Yeah, maybe that's why Rick's such a spoiled brat. He's got too much money."

"Goodness," said Mabel, "how can you speak like that about your friend?"

"My ex-friend, you mean."

"Oh, poor Jeremy. You don't understand what real friendship is."

"Oh, and I suppose you *do*."

"Well, getting back to fishing," Dotty said, "we simply must go. We have our reasons."

"N-O spells NO!" I said.

Mabel sighed. "You have nothing but this silly box" — she pointed to the TV — "to keep you entertained. What you need is some real entertainment. A fishing trip is just the thing."

A noise in the kitchen gave me the perfect excuse to escape the aunties.

I found my mother listening to country music on the radio and cleaning out the fridge. Obviously something was very wrong.

"What's up?" I said. "You're home from work early."

"I am attempting to cheer myself up," she said sadly. "The theatre has laid off half its employees. I have just lost my job."

"Oh, no," I said. "That's pretty awful." The bad news was sure piling up today. "Just a sec." I went and fetched the piggybank. "For you, Mom."

She took it out of the bag. "Jeremy, what a kind and generous boy you are!"

I smiled.

"If it was a real Cadillac," she said, "we could hop inside and take a road trip to Tennessee or Calgary or someplace. We need a holiday."

"I heard about a nice fishing spot just today. We could go fishing." As soon as the words were out of my mouth I was sorry. I hated fishing.

"Fishing? Great idea! Oh, Jeremy, you're so thoughtful. I'll get changed while you pack the car. I feel better already." She gave me a big hug and a squeeze.

"Pack the aunties too," she said. "They'll add an appropriate nostalgic note to the scene. Did you see the new outfits I chose for them?"

"Very generous and kind and thoughtful of you," I said.

"Don't you like them? I put their old clothes in a box under the couch. You can change them back if you like. Although the new ones are perfect for a fishing expedition. It will be just like a lovely old-fashioned Sunday school picnic."

I carried rods, nets, and folding chairs out to the trunk and set the aunties in the back seat. I drew a little map based on directions they gave me.

"Well, you got your way," I told them. "I hope you know I'm only doing this for my mom."

"My dear boy," Dotty said happily, "we simply *adore* fishing. The trout, and the bass, and the *frogs* we used to catch!"

Gladys sighed. "Why, I haven't tasted fried frogs' legs in — in years."

Frogs' legs? I gulped.

"We've never ridden in an automobile before," Dotty said. "I can hardly wait!"

"You mean there weren't even any cars back when you were — alive?"

"Of course there were," Mabel replied. "But we led respectable lives. We did not hold with such fast contrivances as automobiles and telephones and radio sets. I am afraid dear Dotty inherited her modern ways from her mother's side."

"Oh, Jeremy!" called a voice from across the street. Rick's dad, Professor Ricketts, led by his poodle, Solange, came towards me.

"The aunties look charming. Especially the bathing beauty."

I was sure that Dotty would have blushed in embarrassment if she could have.

"Where are you taking them?"

"Uh, fishing," I muttered, looking at the ground.

Solange was sniffing inside the car, growling.

"Tell me, are you interested in photography, Jeremy?"

"Photography?" I took lousy pictures. In fact, I had broken the camera last Christmas taking the film out. Rick had got a camcorder for his last birthday, while I didn't have even a simple camera.

"I've been doing a little independent research study, since I have the summer off. Local history, that sort of thing. Just for fun, you know. Do you know what used to stand where your house is now?"

"No. What?" I had no idea where the conversation was going. Professor Ricketts often talked like this.

"Well, I'll tell you. A photographic studio was erected on this very site sometime before the turn of the century. This was just the outskirts of the city at that time, of course."

"A photo studio?" I repeated. I knew the aunties were listening carefully from the back seat.

"Yes, and a most unusual photo studio too. Unusual in that its owner, a Mr. Fergus Phillips, was the last photographer in Canada to produce portraits using the old tin and copper plate method, which had gone out of style years before."

I shivered, thinking of the aunties' last memory — of a smoke-filled photo studio . . . "What happened to it?"

"Destroyed by fire. Most unfortunate. It could have been a real museum of photographic history."

"When — when was the fire?

"Oh, long before your time, Jeremy. Even before mine. Half a century, give or take."

The aunties had come alive in the exact same place they had died? Maybe the photo had been taken at the very moment they stopped breathing. . . ? It was eerie to think about. But if the old photograph was the thing that had brought the aunties back to life, then maybe my mother did not have any particular magical ability after all. That would be a relief.

"I've collected quite a little bit of information on the subject — books, cameras, the photographer's diary . . . Well, Solange and I must be on our way. Come and see Rick when he gets back. I've missed you around there."

"Back from where?"

"Oh, Rick's spending a week or two at some professional tennis camp up north. A very posh pushy-pooh sort of place. His mother is paying. Good-bye."

"Holy smokes!" I said, when he was gone. "Did you hear that? Does that mean the three of you came alive because you were, like — resurrected — right here on the same spot where you, uh —?"

"We have always been a little curious about that photograph," Dotty said.

"Do you think it's a *magic* photo?"

Mabel sniffed. "Personally, I have never believed in any hocus pocus magic monkey business."

I was going to ask her how she could say that when she herself was living proof of some weird magic monkey business, but just then my mother appeared with the picnic cooler.

"To the fishing hole!" she cried, and we set off with a squeal of tires. I sat in the front seat, crossing my fingers we wouldn't get caught for speeding. The aunties were not wearing seatbelts. Besides having a roof that was permanently stuck halfway down, our old convertible had no seatbelts in the back, no muffler, and no side mirror. It was the sort of car the police loved to pull over.

"You're sure you know where we're going?" my mother asked. "I never heard of a fishing spot so close to — @#!#$!!" She slammed on the brakes and swerved as a black van pulled out of a sideroad right in front of us.

CHAPTER EIGHT

DEEP DIRTY WATER

SOMEHOW WE MANAGED to avoid hitting the van, but our screeching stop sent the three aunties hurtling past the open roof and over the hood. The van sped away. To make matters worse, we could hear a police siren behind us, getting louder and louder. I leaped out of the car to rescue the aunties. They were sprawled in the ditch, shaken, and a bit muddled, but uninjured as far as I could tell. I brushed the dust off their clothes and set them back in the car. A police car squealed to a stop behind us and a policewoman jumped out.

"You folks all right?"

"We're fine," my mother said shakily. "There was no collision. But the driver of that van is a menace! He nearly put an end to our fishing trip! After him!"

"You're sure you're all right?" asked the policewoman. "From a distance it looked like there were bodies strewn all over the road." She took off her sunglasses and peered into the back seat. "Oh!" she said. "Puppets. Ha ha. For a minute there I thought . . . Did you say a black van? Did you see

the driver? Get the licence?"

We shook our heads.

"If it was who I think it was . . ." she began. "Well, they're gone now, and I'm due on duty. Drive carefully now." She got into her car and sped off. We let her get a good start before we continued on, a little more slowly. We stopped at the next roadside store to buy some doughnuts and worms. After only about five more minutes of driving, we reached the place I had marked on my map.

We parked the car on a gravel path by a bridge and, while my mother unloaded the trunk, I carried the aunties through the dusty weeds to a spot where the river widened. The fishing hole was not quite the way the aunties had described it. Around the edge of the pool were several dead willows, a heap of rusty tin cans, and seven or eight abandoned cars. The water smelled of rust and rotten fish.

"Lovely spot," I said, looking around.

The aunties sighed. "It's changed a little since the last time we were here. Still, it is secluded, and the fish we used to catch here were the tastiest, juiciest —"

"Nothing could live in that muck," I said. "I wouldn't touch anything that came out of there."

My mother joined us and eyed the slime-covered pool. "Hmm. Who told you about this place,

Jeremy? It looks like it's seen better days. Oh, well," she added cheerfully, "it's not what you catch that makes fishing so enjoyable. It's the pleasure of sitting in the shade pretending to work while you are in fact relaxing with the newspaper." She propped a fishing line between her knees, took a doughnut from the box, and leaned back against a tree with her newspaper open like a big sun screen in front of her.

I went back to the car and got the three lawn chairs for the aunties, skewered worms onto hooks, and gave them each a rod. I watched in amazement as they cast their lines in graceful arcs to the far side of the river. They hadn't lied; they were real professionals. I cast my own line and flopped down on the bank at their feet.

They were impatient fisherwomen, though. They never let their hooks stay in the water, but kept casting and reeling in and casting again.

"It would be better if we had a little rowboat and some big nets," Dotty whispered, "but we'll do the best we can . . ."

"Here's something interesting, Jeremy," my mother said from behind her newspaper. "A picture of those three bank robbers. It says they escaped from jail and robbed a bank and got clean away! Can you believe it?"

I went to look at the picture. There were the

three men we had seen on TV. One had big bristling eyebrows, another a crooked scar on his face. The third had wispy white hair and a hearing aid. They looked mean and dangerous.

"Great-looking gangster-types, eh?" my mother said enthusiastically. "You're so fond of the aunties, perhaps I should make some uncles too. I could base them on these pictures."

"Please," I said firmly, "don't!"

"Good gracious, no!" cried Dotty, forgetting, in her excitement, not to talk in front of my mother. I coughed loudly to cover her words, but my mother didn't seem to have heard anyway.

Something nudged me. It was Gladys's elbow. "I've — got — a — bite," she whispered, nodding towards her line. I jumped up and switched rods with her. She was right; I could feel a strong pull on her line. Then I felt a tug, and a series of sharp jerks as if a very large fish was trying to wiggle off the hook.

"Holy mackerel!" I yelled. "The thing must be massive. It's pulling like crazy." I dug my heels into the bank and held on. The aunties and my mother looked on with interest.

"Help, somebody," I yelled, "before it drags me in!"

My mother dropped her paper and got to her

feet, pointing. "Something came out of the water," she said. "It looked like a — hand. All black and rubbery. I think — you've caught a body, Jeremy."

"I've caught a body?" Suddenly I felt sick to my stomach. I nearly dropped the fishing rod, but a flurry of tugs at the end of the line made me grab it again.

"It's putting up a pretty good fight for a body," my mother said nervously. "I'll help you reel it in."

When my line seemed about to snap, the thing I had caught stopped fighting and swirled towards me. Two large flippers churned the water to spray. Something black bulged out of the algae just in front of us. The creature reached the shallow water by the bank and rose up before us, higher and higher. It panted and groped for shore, collapsing in the weeds at our feet. My mom was shaking with terror. So was I.

Mom gasped in relief. "For pity's sake, Jeremy. You've caught a frogman."

I stared at the thing sprawled at our feet. It was not a sea monster. It was, I could now see, a diver in a black wetsuit, with a mask, a tank, and a diving light. Gladys's hook and worm were tangled around his oxygen line.

"Is he still alive?"

"He's unconscious but breathing. I think," my

mother said. "We'd better get help. You give him mouth-to-mouth. I'll run to the road and flag down some help." She hurried off towards the bridge.

The aunties leaned forward in their lawn chairs.

"I do hope I haven't strangulated the poor creature!" Gladys said.

I removed the diver's mouthpiece to give him artificial respiration, but to our relief his chest moved up and down slightly as he breathed on his own.

"Frogman? He was down there catching frogs?" Dotty asked.

Gladys giggled. "If I kiss him will he turn into a handsome prince?"

"What *is* a frogman?" Mabel asked. "Does your mother actually believe that he is part amphibian?"

"A frogman is a diver," I explained. "Some people dive for recreation, just to see what's under the water. Or they go searching for something — like treasure from shipwrecks. Don't ask me what this guy was doing in that polluted puddle."

"Treasure?" the diver murmured, trying to sit up. A car door slammed and my mother came running through the weeds with the policewoman we'd seen earlier.

"Look who I met on the bridge!" my mother said. "By the wildest coincidence she was parked just on the other side of the river."

"Rod!" the policewoman cried, brushing past us and kneeling beside the diver. "Oh, Roddy! It's Sheila. Are you all right? Did you find anything? What happened?" She pulled off the diver's mask.

Rod opened his eyes and blinked at the three real people and three stuffed people who were all anxiously staring at him. He blinked again and shook his head as if trying to shake away a bad dream. "Oxygen cut off," he mumbled. "Must have got caught on something."

"You're all right now, darling," the policewoman told him. "It was just a fishing rod, Rod." She kissed him smack on the lips. The aunties glanced at each other. Gladys nudged Dotty.

Then the policewoman pulled back the diver's rubber hood. I recognized him immediately. It was the red-haired cop. Fortunately, he was far too muddled to recognize me.

"A police diver?" I asked. "What was he looking for in that pool?"

"It's a police matter," the policewoman said. "I was watching you from across the river. What are *you* doing here?"

"You'd better start packing up, Jeremy," my mother said. "The officer tells me this is private property. We have been trespassing."

Turning to my mother, the policewoman said, "I think I'd better get my partner to a hospital. If you'd kindly take his legs we can carry him to my car."

"Certainly," my mother said. "I feel simply dreadful about all this, officer. It was an accident, I assure you. I don't believe my son has actually ever caught anything before."

My mother picked up Rod's flippers, the policewoman his shoulders, and together they heaved him down the path, around our car, and across the bridge.

"Well, too bad he didn't turn into a prince," Dotty said when they were out of sight.

"Roddy the body was an ugly frog," Gladys said. "Except his legs looked rather plump and juicy." She gave a small snort of laughter.

"Jeremy," Mabel said, "there is something I must tell you. I am afraid there is something on *my* line. I do hope it is not another body, but it does feel suspiciously heavy."

I groaned. "You're probably snagged on a log." Her line stretched nearly to the opposite bank. "You've got my mother's favourite lure on too." I took her rod and gave a few good yanks, but nothing happened. I was afraid the line would snap and I'd lose the lure. I decided to cross the bridge and try to unhook it from the other bank. My mother and the policewoman were fussing over Roddy in the back seat of the unmarked car and hardly noticed me. I could see where Mabel's line was caught. I reached in, shuddering at the thought of all the germy sewage in the pool, and dragged up the thing it was snagged on. It was a dripping burlap bundle about the size of a small suitcase.

I looked across the river at the aunties.

They motioned me to return.

I glanced at my mother and the cops. The water was shallow just below the pool where fallen trees and stuff made a natural dam. I began wading across, carrying the mysterious bundle. Fortunately the water only came up to my knees, and fortunately I had on old tennis shoes.

I dropped the bundle at the aunties' feet.

"Treasure!" Gladys cried. "Even better than a prince! Quick, stow it in the trunk before your mother gets back."

"It looks a little fishy," I said. "Are you sure we should? Hey!" I cried, as a brainwave struck me, "this might be what Rod the police diver was searching for."

"Jeremy, of *course* it is," Dotty said. "We simply must find out what's inside."

"It could be jewels, or weapons, or drugs, like in all the crime shows on TV," Gladys told me.

"How dreadfully exciting!"

"Then shouldn't we turn it over to the police?" I asked.

"Without even checking?" Dotty said. "Don't be a wet blanket, Jeremy, dear."

"Yes, don't be such a stick in the mud," Gladys added.

"At times, dear boy, you are as dull as ditchwater," Mabel said. "Your mother is coming back. Make up your mind."

I scooped up the soggy bundle and pushed it into a corner of the trunk. I laid the folding chairs over it, then seated the aunties in the car.

I didn't know if it was the bundle in the trunk or the thought of another car ride that made them clutch each other nervously and cross their fingers.

"Oh good, you're all ready," my mother said. "Well, I suppose we'd better go — the excitement's all over.

"You know," she added, turning the car onto the highway, "it's lucky we weren't all arrested for interfering in an underwater mission and nearly killing a police officer. I wonder what they were searching for." She sniffed the air. "And what *is* that fishy odour?"

"It might be my feet," I said. "I seem to have got myself into some deep dirty water."

CHAPTER NINE

RETURN TO THE SLIMY HOLE

LATE THAT NIGHT, after my mother had gone to bed, I brought the damp package in from the car and laid it on a pile of newspapers on the living room rug. I sat the aunties in a circle on the floor so they could see better.

"Oh, I do love a good mystery." Gladys rubbed her gloves together. "Maybe it's a bomb!"

"Nonsense," Mabel said, "bombs tick. Of course it is not a bomb. Open it up."

"I don't know," I began. "It's really not ours . . ."

"Finders keepers!" Gladys said. "Maybe it's nothing but an old bag of garbage, or drugs or something. Bombs away!"

I ended up giving in, as usual, and went to fetch a pair of scissors.

"Well, it's been nice knowing the three of you." I cut the string and opened up the burlap bag. Inside lay a small muddy metal box. I hesitated. Jewels, drugs, guns — what would we do with whatever we found inside?

Mabel prodded the box with the tip of her cane and the lid popped off. Inside lay dozens of bundles of brownish paper. It took me a minute to notice the small '100' in the corners. At first I was so stunned I couldn't speak, but then I kind of went nuts.

"We're *rich* !" I gasped, tossing handfuls of hundred-dollar bills into the air. "Rich, rich, rich!" The money floated down and covered us like leaves. "You can buy anything you want now. More clothes, a new couch, a bigger TV. I can buy my mother a new car. She really needs one, and I've always wanted my own computer, and how about a camcorder and an answering machine and a new ten-speed and . . ."

Mabel, Gladys, and Dotty were listening and nodding, fingering and counting the bundles of money.

I looked at them more closely. "Uh, wait a minute," I said. "This money doesn't, uh, really belong to us, does it?"

"It's true you could use a new car," Dotty remarked.

"Your mother," Gladys reminded me, "has just lost her job. If you keep all this money, she'd never have to work again."

"And you are such a poor and underprivileged boy," Mabel said. "Imagine, no computer."

"But we stole the money off private property," I said. "We can't just keep it. We'll have to tell the cops."

"Are you sure, dear boy, that you wish to inform the police?" Mabel said. "Whom do you suppose put that money in the fishing hole?"

"Search me. I suppose some sort of criminals or somebody . . . Oh! Do you mean," I asked in a whisper, "do you mean you think it was —"

Dotty nodded.

"Not — not the Banks Brothers!" I gulped. "Not again! It couldn't be!"

"Judging from their past," Mabel said, "it would not surprise me at all if the Banks Brothers robbed river banks as well as the other kind."

"We know they've escaped again," I said, "and robbed a bank, and the police were watching the river, and then we found all this money in it . . . but that doesn't mean the Banks Brothers put it there. Does it?"

"If they did," said Dotty, "it will be the second time you've been mixed up with the Banks Brothers. It will look a little suspicious, don't you think?"

"It is suspicious." I stared at the aunties. "Did you three know that money was in that fishing hole all the time? You made me take you fishing there because you expected to find it?"

"Bingo," said Gladys. "It took you long enough to catch on."

"But — but how did you know it was there?"

"Simple deduction, dear boy. You heard the news last night. The announcer said the Banks Brothers made their escape on a motorcycle and headed west out of town. It said the police lost their trail near a bridge."

"But it could have been any road going west," I said. "It could have been any bridge, an overpass, or anything."

"Is there more than one road leading west out of town?" Mabel asked. "There wasn't in our day."

"The news report said the motorcycle left the road near a bridge, and the police had not recovered the money," Dotty added. "That made us think the money must be in the water. By the bridge. And we were right!"

"I still don't know how you figured it out." I scratched my head. "It must have been luck. Bad luck. I wish we'd never heard of those Banks Brothers. So I guess we'd better call the cops and tell them we found it."

"Are you bonkers?" asked Gladys. "The cops?"

"You mean you plan to *keep* the money?" It was a scary idea, but in a way I thought I deserved it. The Banks Brothers had cheated me out of my reward by escaping. Maybe I should just keep a thousand or so . . .

"We can't," I said. "It's dishonest. It would be stealing. We'd be criminals!"

"You would only get into trouble if you told the police," Dotty said. "They would never believe you if you told them about our part in it, would they?"

I could see her point. "So we can't keep the money and we can't turn it over to the cops," I said slowly. "What are we supposed to do? Mabel, you don't really think we should keep the money for ourselves, do you?"

"It has nothing to do with Gladys and Dotty and me," Mabel said, gazing into the distance. "You are the one who needs money. Money is of no use to us."

"Although," Dotty added, "a bigger TV with more channels and a car with a roof would be most pleasant."

"It is your decision," Gladys said. "Though you'd be a bonehead to tell the cops."

"You got us into this mess," I said, "and now you expect me to get us out of it."

I went to the kitchen for a snack. (I hardly ever ate in front of the aunties; it didn't seem polite when they couldn't.) I tried to think straight about this new mess. I was being more honest than the aunties were! If I kept all that money I would be rich — richer than Rick! But keeping the money would really be like stealing. And yet, if I told the cops, they might figure out that the aunties had been involved in these weird adventures. They would force the aunties' secret out of me. And then they'd take the aunties away and lock them up. They would probably lock me up too.

I ate some leftover noodles, a hotdog, and some rhubarb jam. I had to make a decision quickly, before the aunties talked me into something I shouldn't do. I finished the jam and went back to the living room.

"We have been thinking, Jeremy," Mabel began as soon as she saw me. "What we must do now is —"

"Here's the plan," I interrupted. "Wrap the money up. I'm taking it back to the river, where we should have left it. No one will ever know we had it."

"Tonight?" Dotty gasped. "All that way in the dark? Won't you be frightened?"

"Ha! I'm not scared of the dark."

"We would not want you to do anything rash, dear boy," Mabel said slowly.

"We don't want you to do anything at all," Gladys said. "What's the hurry? Hang on to the money until we perfect our plan."

I spoke firmly. "Maybe I'm tired of you and your plans. I can make my own decisions, you know. I am taking the money back to the fishing hole. Right now."

"My, aren't you getting brave!" Gladys said. "Isn't he getting brave, girls?"

"Well," said Mabel. "We cannot stop you if you insist. If you *must* take it back, I suppose the middle of the night is the safest time. Even the police have to sleep sometime."

"You oughtn't to go alone, dear," Dotty worried. "I am sure I could drive your mother's car if you showed me which levers and cranks to turn."

"I'll go by myself," I said firmly. "On my bike." I hoped they were impressed.

"If you feel you are doing the right thing," Mabel said doubtfully. "We will wrap up the money while you get a coat and a flashlight."

"You can borrow my umbrella," Gladys said. "And Mabel's cane. Just in case, you know. Whatever you do, don't get taken alive."

"Very funny," I said.

It took me a while to find my jacket and a flashlight that worked. I burrowed around in the big walk-in hall closet and finally came up with my school jacket, the one with my name on the back, and a Mickey Mouse flashlight I'd had since I was a kid. I almost couldn't get out of the closet. The door sticks and the doorknob has to be twisted and jerked exactly right. My mother's attempts to fix it had only made it worse. When I finally got out, the money was all wrapped up, just as we had found it.

"You know, Jeremy," Gladys said as I went to the door, "you're a new man. You're a different person from the timid little tad we used to know. These adventures show you what you're really made of !"

"Yes," said Dotty, "just like a Real Man. Real Men are tough and fearless outdoorsmen who always try to do the honest thing!" She snickered.

They were all giggling as I went out the door.

At times like this I wondered what it would be like to be rid of the aunties. But how could I get rid of them if I didn't know where they had come from — or why they had come to life in my living room? In a way they were fun, always interesting, and even better than pets — they didn't have to be fed or walked. But they were getting so rude and pushy. I didn't seem to get any privacy anymore — or enough sleep. And they were always getting me into trouble. The thought of sharing the whole rest of my life with them, even when I was an old man, was kind of worrying. I imagined the four of us squeezed onto the couch, me the wrinkliest of all.

As I biked down the street I wondered if maybe the aunties were right, though. Maybe I *was* a different person since meeting them. I could hardly even remember life before they had joined the family. It must have been pretty humdrum. Come to think of it, maybe I *had* become a little braver since they had moved in. Maybe I was even a little more polite. And, compared to them, I was pretty honest too!

It was a dark night, especially where the road went through the bush and there were no street-lights. I was scared out of my wits — who wouldn't be? — but I kept remembering how impressed the aunties would be with my bravery. They had been so bossy lately, I was surprised they had given in so easily for a change. Maybe they were beginning to realize that if it wasn't for me, they wouldn't have such an interesting life. Or any life at all.

I heard an eerie rustling and a mysterious hoot from the woods. If it wasn't for the aunties, I thought, pedalling faster, I wouldn't have such a *dangerous* life!

At last I reached the river and crossed the bridge to the far side where I had found the bundle. Loud croaks came from the weeds nearby. It sounded like monster frogs. Frogs are disgusting. They're so pudgy and slippery, and the way they leap up out of the grass scares the socks off me.

I propped my bike against some bushes, picked up the bundle, and walked cautiously towards the river, shining my flashlight in front of my sneakers in case of lurking leapers. I was so busy watching my feet I nearly walked into a car! I threw myself down in the weeds, praying I hadn't been heard. I crouched in the grass, not daring to move. My heart was pounding. I waited a long time. Nothing happened. I risked a quick flash of my light. I couldn't see anyone in the car. What I could see was a red light. On the roof. A cop car! The fishing hole was still being watched!

The frogs were croaking all around me. I could pick out two separate froggy voices. One went *Crooooaaaak — rib rib rib ribbet snork*. The other went *Aaaaaaah — croak! Aaaaaaah — croak!* Weird frogs. Maybe they were mutated — from all the pollution in the fishing hole. But the longer I listened, the more it seemed that the frog noises were coming from inside the car. Mutant frogs in a cop car? I slowly raised myself up and peered in the window. Two cops were sound asleep, snoring their heads off! *Aaaaaaah — croak! Rib rib rib ribbet snork*! I crept away towards the river bank with the burlap bundle, trying not to giggle.

"Stop right there!" growled a voice behind me.

CHAPTER TEN

THOSE AUNTIES ARE UP TO SOMETHING

I WAS TOO TERRIFIED to turn around, and shaking so much I could hardly keep my grip on the bundle. It fell to the ground with a thump.

"That's it, sonny, now leave the bag and keep walking," growled the voice. "Don't turn around and you won't get hurt."

Something seemed odd. On TV at least, a cop would not tell you to walk away. But if it wasn't the police, who was it?

I turned my head. There was only one person in the darkness behind me, a man with his hat pulled low and his coat collar turned up around his face.

"Just keep on walking and don't get yourself mixed up in other people's business," he ordered.

He had one hand in his pocket. A gun? Was he a plainclothes policeman or —

"You're just a kid. What's your name, sonny?"

"It's, uh — Rod," I said. "Rod, uh — Diver. What's yours?"

I didn't expect him to answer, but he said, "Banks

is the name and banks is the game, but you can call me Eddy."

My teeth began to chatter. The aunties had been right!

"Ever hear of me?" he asked.

"No, n-n-never." If he realized I was the same person who had led to his last arrest he would hurl me head-first into the fishing hole.

"Ah, well, I'm getting old, I guess. I used to be famous — everyone knew the name of Banks." His voice became businesslike. "Now let's have that bag, sonny."

I must be nuts, pretending to be brave to impress three stuffed dolls. Why had the aunties let me come all alone? They should have guessed there would be danger. They should have warned me. If the aunties were here they would probably have a plan. No way would they just hand over the money to a Banks Brother. I took a step towards the bundle on the ground between us and put my foot on it.

"This isn't your money," I said shakily. "I'm not going to give it to you."

"Ah, so you know there's money inside, do you?" He chuckled grimly.

I could have kicked myself. "Well, yes," I said nervously. "How would you like it if I called the cops over here?"

Eddy Banks did not even glance at the police car. "Sonny, if you'd wanted to call the cops you'd have done it long ago. Besides, you've opened the stash here. Your fingerprints will be on the money, eh? No, you don't want to call the cops."

My shoulders slumped.

"Look, sonny," Eddy Banks said, "I owe you, eh? You saved me the trouble of fishing around in that slimy hole to find the stash. How much do you want?" He took a jack-knife from his pocket and knelt down to slit the bag.

"No, no," I said quickly, "I don't want any."

"Why not? Plenty here," he said. "You deserve it. How did you find the bag? I thought only the cops were on to me. You keep funny hours for a kid," he added. "What do you plan to be when you grow up? You training for a cop or a robber?"

"N-neither — "

"Look, I'll level with you, sonny." He bent closer and whispered confidentially. "This money came from a bank!"

Either I was dreaming or caught in the middle of some phony TV comedy. The only difference was that I was much too scared to laugh.

"Yessir," he said, "that's my hard-earned life savings you're looking at."

"R-really?" I tried to sound innocent.

"That's right. Took me years of hard work to get this much. You see, sonny, I've got two brothers, and the three of us, ah, were doing a little banking the other day —"

"Banking?"

"You know, a simple little withdrawal. But I got into a bit of trouble."

"A bit of trouble?" I echoed weakly.

"Yeah. I kinda got overdrawn. You know how sticky these banks are. I shoulda had some of that overdraft protection, huh? You'd think someone named Banks would know all about banks, but they change the rules so often an old fellow gets con- fused."

Was Eddy trying to be funny? He looked serious and mean.

"Right, so we're making this withdrawal, see, and there's this little problem. Seems we were there too early. Bank wasn't supposed to be open yet. Anyone can make a mistake, and as they say, the early bird catches the worm, eh? Well, Sonny, we got caught all right. I mean, detained for questioning. We thought this was unfair, so when they weren't look- ing, we left. It was banking hours by then, so we went back to the bank, got our money, and took off on a motorcycle we borrowed off a stranger."

Part of me wanted to point out that borrowing

from a stranger was stealing. Part of me didn't want to end up in the fishing hole. "Yes, it was on TV," I said.

Eddy took a step closer. "I thought you said you never heard of me, sonny."

"Uh, I-I never caught the name," I stammered. "It was j-just a news flash after they said about me being the observant young —" I bit down hard on my tongue. "Then what?" I asked in a small voice.

"Some crazy off-duty cop must have thought we were speeding or something and followed us outa town. I dunno. I must be getting old. Those high-speed chases aren't as thrilling as they used to be. It was downright dangerous. I was driving, my little brother, Harv, was on behind, and my big brother, Mort, was in the sidecar with the loot. I don't know how it happened, but somehow I lost control on a curve and we went skidding down the bank there by that bridge and right into this here river!"

"What about the bike?" I asked.

"Junked it," Eddy said. "We've got Black Betty now, a fancy van, on loan from a friend we haven't met yet. She's a real beaut."

"W-what about the cops?"

Eddy chuckled. "Lost 'em. By the time they realized we'd taken a spill in the drink, we were out again, watching from the weeds. Only we never found the money, and those crazy cops have been watching the place two nights running. You'd think they had better things to do than worry about three old fellows making a banking boo-boo. So thanks again, sonny. I'm real indebted to you for your kindness." He bent down to pick up the bundle.

"Wait," I said. "What are you planning to do with all that money?"

"Oh, little operation. Gotta keep it close to the chest," he whispered, patting his chest.

"All that for an operation? I thought the government pays for chest operations."

"Oho, you don't know the kind of operation I mean. Let's say it's for my poor sick old momma. Got to get her heart bypass surgery, that's it! Bypassing hearts is just part of life for us Banks. So you see, this money's a matter of life and death, sonny. Don't gimme any trouble."

Should I let him have the money? Would his mother really die? He was so old, could his mother even still be alive? He had a knife, maybe a gun. But what would the aunties say if I told them I'd just handed the money over?

"You're lying!" I said. "You can't fool me. You're nothing but a lying bank robber!" I gave the bundle a flying kick, and I heard a soft splash and a loud curse. As I raced past the police car, the interior light was on and I could see Rod and Sheila sitting up rubbing their eyes. I grabbed my bike and pedalled for home fast enough to win Olympic gold.

The sun was rising as I slipped into the house. I could hear my mother clattering pots and pans as she made breakfast, and an unpleasant buttery smell came from the kitchen. I tiptoed into the living room.

The aunties seemed relieved to see me. I told them everything.

"The police *and* the Banks Brothers?" they gasped. "Dear boy, we never should have let you go!"

"He came out of nowhere," I concluded. "I couldn't help being seen."

"We were right, you see," Gladys said. "You ought to trust us. The money *was* lost there by the Banks Brothers, those vile, vicious villains! Did he really expect you to swallow that story about banking errors and chest operations?"

"Thank goodness Mr. Banks did not get that bundle!" Dotty said. "I wish I could have seen his face when the bag splashed into the river."

"He did not get the bundle, that is the main thing," Mabel said. "And, of course, it was nice that you got away safely too."

Gladys and Dotty nodded. All three of the

aunties looked uneasy.

"What's up?" I asked.

"Oh, nothing, nothing."

"What were you talking about when I was gone?"

"Nothing, nothing at all. Just waiting," Gladys said.

"Well, I'm glad I took the money back," I said. "I'm sure you see now that it was the honest thing to do."

The aunties were too proud to apologize. They could not admit that I had been right for a change.

"I don't plan to get mixed up with the police again," I said. "Once was enough."

"The police are wet brains," Gladys said, "when it comes to catching crooks. We could do a better job of catching the Banks Brothers than they could."

"Ha!" I said. "You can't even walk."

"What does that have to do with it? There is no need to chase the Banks Brothers. Money is the key to their hearts. They must be lured into a net, not chased." Dotty and Mabel nodded.

I was just glad to be home. I never wanted to get involved with crooks or cops again in my life.

"I feel very strange," I said, aware of my empty stomach and buzzing head. I hadn't eaten or slept in hours.

Mabel sighed. "We would have told you, dear boy, of our plans, but we did not wish to alarm you unnecessarily."

I eyed them. "What's going on?

"Oh — then you *don't* know." Dotty sounded relieved.

"What are you three keeping from me?" I asked. "All the while I was gone you were sitting here making plans behind my back, were you?"

Gladys grinned. "Next time we'll be sure to make them in front of your back."

"What's going on?" I demanded. "You can't keep secrets from me. I *made* you."

"Excuse *me*," Mabel said stiffly, "do you think that merely because you made us we can have no ideas of our own?"

"Okay, I know I didn't really *make* you. But you can't keep things from me. It's not fair."

"It's only a little plan of ours," Gladys said. "We would have told you, but you're such a nervous, squeamish chap."

After I had gone back to the fishing hole all alone in the dark and outwitted Eddy Banks, the aunties still thought I was a coward? I glared at them. "I am not squeamish!"

"But you turn green at the mere mention of a little thing like — frogs' legs." Gladys snickered.

"That's squeamish."

I was about to argue, but my mother called from the kitchen: "Jeremy? You up? I've got a real treat for breakfast this morning. Since we didn't catch anything yesterday, I got something at the market."

Fish? For breakfast? My appetite disappeared.

"Gourmet frogs' legs!" my mother announced triumphantly.

My stomach heaved. "I think I'll skip breakfast this morning," I called. "I think I'll take a short nap."

"A nap? You just got up." I heard my mother murmur that something fishy was going on when a healthy boy slept in one day till four o'clock and another day needed a nap before seven in the morning. I had to agree. Something fishy was going on. But what? I turned back to the aunties.

"There's something about that money or the Banks Brothers that you're not telling me, isn't there? You can't fool me."

"What are you, dense?" Gladys said rudely. "Obviously we just *did* fool you or you wouldn't have made that remark."

I was too tired to argue.

"Have a little sleep, dear boy," Mabel said. "We shall tell you all when you have had some rest."

"Yes, you look like you're about to croak,"

Gladys added, and all three giggled as I went up the stairs. Sometimes Mabel, Gladys, and Dotty were infuriating.

I was so tired I had a hard time drifting off, but when I finally did, my sleep was disturbed by a weird and vivid dream. We were back at the fishing hole. The water was clear as an aquarium. You could see right to the bottom. There was nothing in there except three mermaids, who were the three aunties. They splashed and swam around, quite excited at the way they were able to get around without my help. They had long fish tails and they were wearing the top parts of their usual outfits. They were busily fishing for frogs with their hairnets. The three Banks Brothers were also there, at least in part: their three pairs of legs were dancing around on shore in green striped trousers. They were showing off dance steps and frog kicks. A photographer was going around with an old fashioned movie camera trying to capture the aunties on film.

"Hold that pose," he cried in a thick Scottish accent. "I want to prreserrve ye forr eterrnity!

Wherre arre ye, laddie?" he called, looking around for me. I was standing right beside him. "I canna seem to get a picturre of ye. Wherre arre ye, lad?"

"Right here!" I said.

"Well, I canna see ye. Can ye make yourrself a wee bit denserr?"

"I'm not dense," I said tiredly. "I'm just very very tired."

I lay down on the river bank and tried to fall asleep, but the three wrinkled mermaids rose from the water and sang a song that went something like this:

Swim swim swim — look at him
Something's fishy, how we wish he
Had a little more sense.

Hop hop hops — legs without tops
When we catch the three Banks on
their six shanks
We'll be a little less tense.

Splash splash splashes— camera flashes
He'd figure it out without a doubt
If he were a little less dense.

Even in my dreams the aunties were rude and sarcastic. I growled a bad word at them, but as usual they refused to listen to me.

CHAPTER ELEVEN

THE END OF A SHORT FRIENDSHIP

I WOKE UP a little after lunch. There was a note on the kitchen table with a submarine sandwich and some chocolate chip cookies.

> Dear Jeremy,
>   I did not want to wake you. You were snoring loud enough to wake the dead when I checked you at lunchtime. I am going out job-hunting and will be back at five.
>   Love, Mom xoxo

I ate the sub and nine or ten cookies and went into the living room.

"Here he is at last," Gladys said. "Be seated and we will tell you all."

"All what?" I asked.

"We said we would tell you our secret when you woke up."

"What? You mean you've figured out the reason you're able to talk and everything?"

"No, no, no," Gladys said. "We've decided to tell

you the secret plan we were keeping from you."

"Oh." I yawned. "Well it's about time." I didn't want to seem too interested.

"Well" — Mabel made a peculiar fuzzy sound, as if she was trying to clear her throat — "we are afraid, Jeremy, that you did not exactly return the money to the fishing hole."

"Of course I returned it. I kicked it back into the water before Eddy Banks could get it."

"Well, er, as a matter of fact," Mabel stammered, "actually we, ah —"

"What Mabel is trying to say," Gladys interrupted, "is that while you were out of the room looking for your coat, we replaced the money with a stack of your mother's magazines and rewrapped the tin box. It was not quite the same weight, but we had to decide quickly on a replacement that would not be missed from the house."

"What? You sent me back to that fishing hole knowing I might run into the Banks Brothers," I said angrily. "If Eddy had looked in that box and found a stack of fashion magazines I'd have been dead meat! Thanks a whole lot!"

"We try to keep life interesting for you." Gladys's lips twitched.

"It's not funny!" I shouted. "Now you've really done it. I'm an accessory to a major bank theft! What will the cops say when I tell them it was all your idea? I'm going to end up in jail thanks to you three!"

Had they stashed the money in their clothing? Inside the couch cushions? It must be somewhere in the room. Since the fishing expedition, the aunties hadn't moved off the couch. As far as I *knew*, that is.

"So where did you hide the money?" I asked. "No, wait, don't tell me. It's probably better if I don't know." I stomped out of the room without another word.

For the next few days I avoided the living room. I couldn't even look at the aunties without getting mad. I spent all my time wondering whether I should call the cops and confess everything or find the money and take it back to the fishing hole. I was too scared to do either.

It rained for three days straight. With my mom out of work and at home all the time the house felt small and crowded. I had been planning to practise my tennis serves with Scooter down at the park courts — I did not want to be beaten to a pulp when Rick got back from his professional camp — but the rain put an end to that plan. I phoned up Mark, but he had cousins visiting. I couldn't mow any lawns because the grass was too wet. I couldn't even watch TV because it would have meant sitting in the same room with those aunties. I wished I had never seen their wrinkled old faces.

That's when I remembered the diary. Professor Ricketts had said something about having the photographer's diary at his house. It seemed like a good idea to go and get it. Maybe I'd find out something about that tintype. Like how it had come to life. Anyway, I had to do *something* to take my mind off the three thieves in my living room.

Rick answered the doorbell.

"What are you doing here?" I asked.

"I live here."

"I thought you were at tennis camp."

"Too rainy. Slippery courts. I came home."

"Uh, I need something from your dad."

Professor Ricketts came out of his study just then.

"Hello, Jeremy. Good to see you. How are your aunties doing these days?"

I knew it was just a friendly joke, but with Rick standing right there, I didn't know how to answer without sounding dumb.

"Not giving you any trouble, I hope?" Professor Ricketts smiled.

"Trouble? The aunties? Why would the aunties be giving me trouble?" I managed to squeeze out a sick-sounding laugh. "There's no trouble going on over at my place, none at all. I just came over to see if I could borrow that diary you said you had. The old photographer's."

Professor Rickett's looked a little puzzled, but he went to get it for me. Rick kept standing there, not saying anything. I shuffled my feet. I knew if I said one word I'd be laughed right out of the house.

If only I could prove to Rick that the aunties really could talk. I needed him to help me figure out what to do about the money. I had lost my best friend over an argument about dolls! It was all the aunties' fault. They had ruined my summer. Maybe my whole life.

"I hear Solange was growling at the aunties," Rick said finally. "As if they were ghosts or something."

Was he really interested, or was he just leading up to some rotten Anti-joke? I was saved by his father's return.

"Here you go, Jeremy." He handed me a thin book with a red leather cover. "It was on Rick's bed, of all places! Solange must have dragged it in there. Totally indecipherable, most of it. I believe old Fergus Phillips was a little off his tripod in later years."

"What?"

Professor Ricketts pointed to his head. "Senile.

Bats. Cuckoo. Bit of a mad scientist type. His diary makes very little sense."

"Oh. Well, thanks, anyway." I knew anything I said would make *me* sound bats too. I grabbed the diary and took off.

When I got home, I went straight up to my room. I sat at my desk, staring at the diary, half afraid to open it. What if I actually found out how the aunties had got into my living room? What if I found out how to zap them back to where they'd come from? Life would get back to normal and I wouldn't have any problems.

Slowly I opened the diary that had belonged to the last person to see the aunties alive.

What I saw was a mess of smudgy, smeary scrunched-up scribbles, written two rows per line on the brittle yellowed pages. Fergus Phillips had terrible handwriting, and even when I could make out a few words, they sounded like the confused memories of a person who was not exactly all there.

Most of the book consisted of rows and rows of numbers, and short phrases like "3/4 copper chloride X 2c 3 seconds, light metre at 8" or "tried CO_2 copper sulphide in 5/9 2/3 1/1 and 1/2 ratios zinc no luck."

Were these the formulas of a photographer or the magic spells of a wizard? A few goosebumps popped out on my skin. I read on.

"Electro-magnetic field still too weak," "3/4 Z N. K 39. 096, 87Vi?," "amt of light & timing crucial to movement; 54 Xe." After about twenty pages of stuff like that I was getting good at figuring out his handwriting. But I wasn't learning much.

Then at the end the pages started getting much harder to read. One had nothing but the date and the word "FIRE" scrawled on it in big letters. The last two pages were the most interesting of all:

My work is over. Not finished. Over. My work — my life! One day I am moments away from realizing a dream that will change the world. Moments from the greatest achievement in the history of mankind. To project a living moving form through time and space, anywhere, at any time — this was the dream that went up in smoke. The next day I awaken in a nursing home, with bandages on my hands and eyes, and discover that months have passed! They tell me everything was destroyed in the fire except me and my camera. They thought I would never live, never work, never see again! My records, my materials, my lenses, films and files — everything gone! All that remains to mock me is this diary of my years of struggle. When I rant and rave at the nurses, they whisper, "Poor soul, his mind is gone." The last thing I recall is the smell of smoke, and then a deafening explosion. They tell me they thought I was dead when they pulled me from the flames. Even now, when the bandages are finally off my eyes and I can see, my burnt fingers ache to hold this pen. They tell me I'm lucky. I keep asking about the three ladies. What ladies? they say, insisting there was no one but me in the studio. They think I am mad. Perhaps I am.

They show moving pictures in the lounge here every Friday evening. "Silent movies," they call them. I am too feeble to attend. And why should I? Why should the pictures not come here to my room where I could watch them alone?

Some said I should have contented myself with the simple magic of the photo itself. But how could I, when I know how much more is possible? To project a human likeness where and when I wished, conquering time and space — this was my life's dream!

Perhaps there will be one to follow in my footsteps, trace my path the hard way. Others have tried before, are trying even now. Some are very close to the secret. But theirs are small dreams, their visions condensed in little cabinets. Only I, working alone with my unique method, dreamed of the large free vision. I know it is possible! Though I am finished, my dream will not die — to transcend time and place, so that the past can live forever!

I was shivering so much my glasses were bouncing on my nose. For a long time I sat there shaking. I knew I was the only person on earth who knew that the aunties were the three women mentioned in the diary. Rick had no idea what a strange book had been lying around his house. Had Fergus really been experimenting with recreating life from a photo — transforming tintypes into ghosts? He sure had been up to something pretty weird in that studio of his. I wished I were better at math. Numbers have always confused me. If I were the scientific type I could spend the next few years studying physics and chemistry and photography and figure out exactly what Fergus had done. Maybe I could even do it myself. Or undo it.

Becoming the world's next mad photographer didn't really appeal to me though. I thought it might be a good idea to destroy the diary so no one else would ever get any ideas about fooling around with such dangerous stuff. But I wanted to read it all again. I had the feeling there was something in it I'd missed. Something that somehow must make some sense.

Should I tell the aunties about the diary? I made a quick decision. They had kept things from me. I could keep things from them.

CHAPTER TWELVE

A TRIP TO THE THEATRE

I CONTINUED TO AVOID the aunties. The rain had not let up. Things were getting pretty boring. Scooter went up to his cottage and Mark went to camp. There was nothing to do. That afternoon I made myself a peanut butter and mayo sandwich and sauntered into the living room, ignoring the aunties. My mother was in there reading Help Wanted ads in the newspaper.

"Hi, stranger," she said. "What have you been up to lately? How about a bite?"

I gave her half my sandwich. We have a lot of the same tastes. I switched on an old western.

"You spend so much time watching TV you have no time for your friends, Jeremy," my mother remarked. "Before you know it you won't have any anymore."

I didn't bother to answer that it was the aunties who had lost me my best friend, and that at the moment the TV was my only friend.

I suddenly realized I was stretched out on the floor in front of the TV. Weird. Normally there wasn't enough space to stretch out, the room was so full of theatre props and things. But they had all disappeared. The living room looked almost bare.

"What did you do with all the stuff?"

"Took it back to theatre. Since I'm no longer employed there, they asked me to bring everything back, right down to the last screwdriver. What kind of a way to run things is that? Miserly. I predict they'll be closed before the summer's out. No sense of business, laying off all their best people!" After awhile she went out, mentioning some errands she had to do.

From my place on the rug I could hear the aunties fussing and fidgeting behind me, criticizing my choice of movie, my laziness, my taste in snacks, et cetera, et cetera. I totally ignored them. Then they started discussing whether or not the Real Man is also the Ideal Man. I turned up the volume to drown out their dumb discussion, but they didn't seem to get the hint.

"The Ideal Man," Mabel told Dotty and Gladys, "must be taught respect, courtesy, loyalty, and honesty at an early age, or he will very likely turn into a criminal."

"Or worse — a game show host!" Gladys cried.

The three of them giggled loudly.

"Do you *mind*?" I said. "I'm trying to watch a show." It was a good one too. The cowboys were getting the worst of it in a saloon shoot-out.

"In addition," Dotty said in a slightly quieter voice, "I feel that the Ideal Man should be generous, sociable, dependable, and of course brave."

"He should also be intelligent and imaginative," Gladys added, "and have a good sense of humour as well as a pleasing physique — if you know what I mean." They snickered again.

Disgusting, I thought.

A commercial came on then, so I turned around and said, "What do you three know about men? Especially real men? You should talk. You're not even real women. Since when are you experts? I suppose you think you're perfect or something."

"Why do you think we never married?" Gladys inquired. "Because, dear boy, the ideal man does not exist."

"Of course we don't think we are perfect, Jeremy dear," said Dotty. "We have our little vices just like everyone else."

Little vices? What was stealing?

"I, for instance, used to dearly love a smoke now and then." Dotty glanced sadly at her empty cigarette holder. "I was wondering if perhaps you might buy me a pack, Jeremy. Oh, just to place in the holder. I wouldn't light them. I can't inhale, of course — goodness! I might ignite myself!"

"Certainly not!" I said. "Smoking's bad for your health. And besides, it's *illegal* for someone my age to buy cigarettes."

"Times have changed." Dotty sighed.

"I'm not always perfect either," Gladys confessed in a lowered voice. "I'm afraid I used to delight in — cursing! I nearly got thrown out of the church choir, once, didn't I, Mabel? I was quite noted for my originality. It requires great self-restraint to keep this talent under control."

"I'm afraid I used to bet on the races, when I could afford it," Mabel admitted. "And all three of us enjoyed our drop of sherry now and then. No, Jeremy, we know we are not perfect. Even now. For one thing, we enjoy TV far too much. Of course, there was no TV in our day . . . So very strange, watching someone else's adventures through a window in a little box . . ."

By this time the commercial was over and my show was back on. "Okay, okay," I said. "I watch too much too. But if it's all right with you, I'd like to *hear* it too."

The aunties didn't seem to realize I was mad at them. Worse yet, they didn't even seem to realize that stealing money was a crime. I suppose they thought it was okay as long as you stole from robbers. But they didn't have to worry. I was the one who would get in trouble over it.

The bad guys were just about to hold up a dance hall. Their horses were galloping, their lassoes were whirling, when Mabel poked me with her cane.

"Ahem, Jeremy," she said in a strange voice. "Gladys and Dotty and I have a little problem we would like to tell you about."

"Not now." I kept my eyes on the screen.

"Jeremy, there is a rather important matter we feel we must discuss with you immediately."

"Sit on it." The hold-up was in full swing. The cowboys were just about to rope and tie the sherriff. Suddenly the screen went blank. I turned and glared at the aunties. Sure enough, Gladys was holding the remote.

"I'm sitting on it." She stuffed the remote under her large bottom where I couldn't get at it. "I turned it off because you *must* listen, Jeremy. Mabel has some urgent news."

"This better be good," I said angrily.

"I assure you it is," Mabel said. "Gladys and Dotty and I would like to go to the theatre. Today, if possible."

"You have got to be kidding. If you think I'll take the three of you to a theatre, you must be crazy."

"No need to be rude about it," Gladys said.

"I'm never taking you anywhere ever again after

what you did! Stealing the money, hiding it, sending me back to the fishing hole in the middle of the night!"

"It was your idea to go back to the fishing hole," Mabel said.

"Why did you keep the money and trick me like that? You said yourselves that money is of no use to you."

"We thought you'd never ask," Gladys said. "It's very simple. We need the money to lure the Banks Brothers here so we can capture them. Don't you want that reward? We couldn't just return the money to the river and let the silly cops get all the glory, could we? We would have told you our plan sooner if you had not gone out of your way to avoid us these last few days."

I stared at the aunties. "What makes you think the Banks Brothers will know *we've* got the money? How on earth will they track us down?"

"Simple," Gladys replied. "How many boys do you think there are in this city with red hair, freckles, glasses, and their name written on the back of their coat?"

"Oh no! I forgot about my coat! Why didn't you tell me?"

Gladys shrugged. "We couldn't be sure the Banks Brothers would see your coat. But the subscription labels on the magazines we put in the tin box had this address on. If the Banks Brothers weren't so stupid, they could have found us already."

"I don't want them coming here!" I yelled. "We could get into all kinds of trouble. We could be in real danger! You could have at least asked me!"

"We would have, Jeremy," said Dotty, "but we were sure you would not agree with us."

"You're right about that! I never heard of such a crazy plan! This is all just another trick, isn't it? You're bored and you want a little outing, don't you? A little bike ride around town."

"Jeremy," Dotty said, "we would *never* trick you unless it was absolutely necessary. We are telling the truth. Cross our hearts and hope to die."

Each of them solemnly placed a glove on her chest. Some promise.

"So where did you hide the money?" I asked.

"Underneath us," Mabel said calmly.

"You mean you're sitting on it?"

"No," said Mabel. "I mean that we put it under the couch, in the box where your mother stored the clothes we had on before we got these new ones."

"Great! Just great!" I snarled. "There are thousands, maybe hundreds of thousands of dollars of stolen money in a cardboard box under my living room couch!"

"Not exactly," Mabel said. "There *used* to be a box of stolen money under the couch. But a few days ago your mother returned all the things that belonged to the theatre, including that box of costumes. That is why we must go to the theatre. We must get that money back here."

"Well, I'm glad the money's out of this house. You better cross all your fingers the Banks Brothers never find us. If what you say is true, it's a good thing the money *is* at the theatre."

"But, Jeremy," Dotty said, "we feel very strongly that we must go to the theatre and bring the money back here."

"Are you *nuts* ? It was bad enough to steal it once. I refuse to steal it twice."

"Suppose the Banks Brothers track us down and we *do not* have the money here," Mabel said. "What do you suppose they would do to us?"

"Suppose someone finds the money at the theatre," Gladys said. "In a box delivered there by your mother. Can you imagine the trouble she would be in?"

"I suppose you have a point," I said very slowly. "Maybe the money would be safer here than at the theatre, but —"

"Then you agree we are right as usual," Gladys said. "Let's get going. It will be so exciting."

"I do not agree that you're right. What you want to do is wrong!"

I flipped through the channels by hand, looking for another movie. At least TV adventures were nice and safe, and always ended on the hour. I didn't feel ready for any more crazy real-life adventures with the aunties.

"Do please listen to us. You must trust us, Jeremy," Dotty said. "You must put yourself in our hands."

I looked at the aunties' limp gloved hands.

"Do you not believe, my dear boy," Mabel asked, "that we have your best interests at heart? We would never endanger your life unnecessarily."

I bet. They didn't *have* hearts, and they'd endangered my life a couple of times already.

But maybe it *was* a good idea to bring the money home where we could keep a sharp eye on it. At this time of day the theatre would be pretty empty. I could probably slip in unnoticed. I knew I had to do the right thing. Even if it was the wrong thing.

"Okay," I said finally. "It looks like I've got no choice."

"Dear Jeremy!" Dotty said. "We knew we could count on you. Now tell me, what are the fashionable set wearing to the theatre these days? It's been so long."

"Raincoats," said Gladys. "It's pouring outside."

I knew the aunties must consider our mission urgent to risk a bike trip through the rain. They were terrified of getting wet. While they got busy making ponchos and hoods out of green garbage bags, I took some of my money out of the couch cushion and went to buy a few supplies for our expedition. When I got back, I helped the aunties on with their raingear and strapped them to my bike. They were all coming. I didn't have the energy for an argument, and besides, I now had reinforced bike tires.

I felt like a cycling garbage man as I pedalled through the streets surrounded by lumpy green bags. The bag in the carrier, Gladys, insisted on having her red-flowered umbrella up, which made it almost impossible for me to see where we were going.

The theatre was a large old building with peeling pink paint. The first-floor windows were boarded up, and a sign above the entrance read: "CLOSED TEMPORARILY"

"So I suppose you're planning another break-and-enter." I sighed loudly. "There's another door around the back, off an alley."

"Good," Gladys said. "I prefer a little privacy when I pick padlocks."

I parked the bike next to a row of garbage cans in the alley. The lock was no problem. A few flicks of Mabel's trusty hairpin, and the door swung open.

CHAPTER THIRTEEN

IN SEARCH OF LOST LOOT

I CARRIED THE AUNTIES inside and shut the door behind us. We were in a dark narrow hallway, lit by a small window above a staircase at the other end. There was a door halfway down the hall, and a stack of old lumber near the stairs. I had used this entrance before, with my mother, but everything looked different now, dim and abandoned.

"Where's the lightswitch?" I felt along the wall. "We'll never find the money in the dark."

"Here." Dotty flicked the switch. Nothing happened. "The electricity must be disconnected. But we know you're not afraid of the dark, Jeremy, are you?"

"You brought the supplies for this trip," Mabel said. "Where are the flashlights?"

"I hope you remembered disguises too," Dotty said.

"And weapons," Gladys said. "We need weapons to defend ourselves in case we're caught in the act."

"Very funny," I said. The aunties watched too many cop shows. I opened the bag and took out the supplies I had bought: twenty metres of yellow clothesline, four chocolate bars, and three pairs of rollerskates.

The aunties stared in disappointment. "Skipping rope?" Mabel said at last. "Rollerskates? Chocolate? This is not a children's party, dear boy."

"Did you really think I was going to *carry* the three of you around this place?" I said. "You'll have to skate. This is the tow-rope. The chocolate is for energy. This stuff cost nearly thirty bucks. Our search better be worth it."

"You know very well we cannot walk," Mabel said, as though I'd insulted her. "It seems to me that rollerskates are a foolish waste of money."

"I suppose you bought them so you could laugh at us falling upon our rumps," Gladys said.

"I just adore the rollerskates!" Dotty said. "I always wanted a set of wheels. Such stylish colours. Jeremy, do help me on with them, won't you?"

They were the plastic kind, yellow, orange, and blue. I strapped a pair onto each auntie.

"Don't worry," I said. "I've got it all figured out. You can do it." I propped the aunties up in a row and doubled the rope around behind them, once under their armpits and once around hip level. It was a challenge, but with a little practice, they were able to balance by holding onto the rope on either side of them. With the two ends in my hand, I walked slowly down the hall. The aunties coasted along behind me, holding their breath. Our trial cruise took us to the stack of lumber by the stairs and back again.

"Well, I'll be! This is fun!" Gladys exclaimed, daringly removing one hand from the rope to wave at me. "Faster, Jeremy!"

"It's like flying," Dotty gasped. "I'm a bird. I'm a plane. I'm an eight-wheeled speed demon!"

"A marvellous idea, Jeremy," Mabel said forgivingly. "Worth every penny. But business before pleasure, girls. We are here for a purpose." She reached out and opened the door we were passing. Dotty and Gladys pulled themselves along the rope to join her. The door opened to the theatre lobby, empty except for a ticket booth and the main staircase. Something moved by my foot. I leapt back and bumped into Mabel, who bumped into Dotty, who bumped into Gladys, and down they went like dominoes, flat on their backs, their skate wheels spinning in the air.

"It was only a mouse," Gladys said from the floor. "What did you think it was, a Banks Brother?"

"Don't tell me you weren't s-scared too! How did you talk me into this insane plan?"

"What is there to be scared of?" Gladys asked. Then, lowering her voice, she added, "Unless, of

course, the Banks Brothers are using this abandoned building as their hideout. But that's why we brought you, Jeremy. You're so brave!"

"Do — do you really think they might be? I mean, hiding out here?"

"Don't be afraid, Jeremy. We'll protect you," Dotty said kindly.

"If I thought the Banks Brothers were here, do you think I'd have come?" I cried. "You tricked me. This whole thing is all your fault!"

"Don't get your bowels in an uproar," Gladys said. "Pull yourself together and lead on. It's do or die, Jeremy. Or would you rather go back home?"

I turned my back on the three of them and gave the rope an extra-hard yank. Going home was a good idea. And if they didn't stop making fun of me, I decided, I *would* go home, and leave them to their fate, alone in a dark theatre. "I don't know how you think we'll find the money in this huge place," I said. "It could be anywhere."

"Where would your mother be likely to leave the box?" Dotty asked.

"Well, there's a props room upstairs."

"Onwards," said Gladys. "We're right behind you."

I thought I would have to carry the aunties one by one up the flight of steps. But the stack of old lumber gave me an idea. On top of the pile lay a long narrow sheet of plywood, perfect for a ramp. I laid it over the steps and set the aunties on it. They arranged their skirts and held onto the rope. I pulled the three of them upstairs backwards.

"Wheeeee!" Dotty let go of the rope at the top of the ramp and whizzed down the slide, shrieking with delight. Gladys immediately followed her example. She put up her red-flowered umbrella and sailed gracefully to the bottom. I had to go all the way back down to get them.

"Look out below!" Mabel called. To my amazement, she came zipping down in a crouch. "Who says you cannot teach an old dog new tricks," she said drily. "Come, girls, take the leash and Jeremy can pull us up again."

"This is not a children's party, remember?" I muttered.

As we went up the steps a second time, Gladys said, "This reminds me of a poem I learned as a child." She began to recite in a hollow voice:

"As I was going up the stair,
I met a man who wasn't there.
He wasn't there again today,
Oh dear, I wish he'd go away."

"Oooh, just like the Banks Brothers." Dotty shivered.

"Shut up!" I said. They were doing it on purpose to bug me. What did they have to fear? I wouldn't be nervous either if I were just a ghost.

At the top of the stairs was another hall with several doors. One by one, I cautiously pushed them open. Two of the rooms were dark washrooms. The third was an office, the fourth a gloomy dressing room, empty except for a big mirror. When I saw our reflections move in it I almost screamed. The aunties gasped. It did not make me feel better to know that they were nervous after all.

The last door, at the end of the hall, led into a pitch-dark area. I stumbled forward and got tangled up in something heavy and suffocating. I think I might have screamed.

Then I heard Dotty say, "We've found the auditorium. This must be the stage entrance. We're behind the scenes — see the curtains? Gracious, I've always wanted to be on the stage!"

Dragging the aunties with me, I crawled under several layers of black curtains until at last we were out on the large stage. We looked out at the rows of empty seats. It was like being in a horror show with no audience.

"L-let's get out of here," I whispered. "What if

the Banks Bothers really are hiding out here. I was crazy to let you talk me into this."

"Ho, ho!" Gladys said. "Why would they be here? The theatre's only been closed a day or two. I was just pulling your leg, dear boy. You fell for it."

"I believe I saw another door somewhere behind those curtains," Mabel said.

Holding the rope, I dragged the aunties back under the curtains and found the door near the back of the stage. I opened it and pulled them after me into the darkness. Suddenly there was nothing under my feet and I felt myself hurtling through space. I landed with a big crash. The aunties fell in a heap on top of me.

"What — what happened?" I rolled over in the darkness, rubbing my head.

"There were stairs on the other side of the door, dear boy," Mabel said. "You missed them."

"Look!" said Dotty. "We've found the props room."

It was a large, crowded room with lots of windows, so at least we could see what we were doing. The walls were lined with wooden backdrops of forests, oceans, and street scenes. There were racks and racks of clothing: pirate and dance costumes, western, Arab, and Japanese costumes. There were also dozens of cardboard boxes!

"This'll take hours," I said. "I'll never find it."

I left the aunties propped against a cupboard and began going through the boxes in search of the one that had been under our couch. They were full of the strangest things: old shoes, plastic vegetables, musical instruments, feathers, dried-up paints, pipes, eyeglasses, wigs, even some *fake* money . . .

I heard a noise behind me. I turned to the aunties — and froze! In their place stood three sinister old cowboys, in ten-gallon hats, drooping moustaches, and leather fringes. The Banks Brothers had found us!

"Howdy, Jeremy," one drawled, and all three burst into laughter.

"Very funny," I said, my heart thumping wildly. "You didn't fool me."

"Yippee-i-o," Gladys said, twirling the tow-rope like a lasso. "We're ready for anything now. Let's catch them ornery critters and rope 'em and tie 'em and throw 'em in the county jail. Giddy-up, horsey."

I turned back to the boxes. The next one I opened was full of old clothes. There was a navy suit, two pairs of old-fashioned underpants, an old fur, a black hat, a sparkly sweater . . . "Hey!" I said. "I think I might have found it!" I shoved back the pile of clothes.

There, in neat stacks, was the money. Hundreds

and hundreds of hundred-dollar bills.

"Geronimo! Eureka! Hooray!" I yelled. "Here it is!"

"Bravo! Congratulations! Well done!" the aunties cried. "Now let's get out of here."

First I made the aunties put back their hats and moustaches.

"We thought you liked cowboys," they grumbled.

I dumped the clothes onto the floor and picked up the box of money. It was not easy retracing my steps through the theatre with three stuffed dolls, a sheet of plywood, and a box full of money. I went first, carrying the ramp, and Mabel coasted along behind me, then Dotty, and last Gladys, dragging the box of money behind her with the curved handle of her umbrella.

"There's not much strength left in these old mitts, but I'm doing my best," she said.

I pulled them back up the stairs to the room behind the stage and out into the hall by the dressing rooms. We hurried down the hallway to the first set of stairs and slid down the ramp to the alley door.

I removed the rope and rollerskates from the aunties. They were still wearing their rain ponchos. With the rope I tied the box up securely, then picked up our supplies bag and the bagged aunties and struggled to the door, weighted down like a pack horse. I padlocked the door behind us, and staggered out into the rain.

Now what? My bike could only carry three dolls maximum, besides me. Why hadn't I thought of this before? There was no room for the box of money. I would have to take everything home in two batches. I stood in the rain wondering who or what to take home first. If I left the money behind, we were back where we started. If I took the money home first, I'd have to leave it alone in the house while I returned for the aunties. I didn't like the idea of the money in an empty house — just in case the Banks Brothers really did show up. And how could I let either Gladys or Dotty or Mabel stay alone at the house or the theatre while I ferried the others home? It was the old problem of the foxes and chickens trying to cross the river. I used to know how to solve that problem. It involved mathematics — not my best subject. I knew if I had a pen and paper I'd probably be able to figure it out eventually. I began tying the box on my rat-trap.

Suddenly Dotty whispered, "Ssst! Police!"

CHAPTER FOURTEEN

SITTING ON A TIME BOMB

"LET'S GO!" Without pausing to look around, I scooped up the aunties and hoisted them astride the bar, noisily knocking over a garbage can in my rush. I threw the supply bag into the carrier, and with one hand steadying the box on the rat-trap, I grabbed a handlebar and started running.

I raced breathlessly down the alley and veered around the corner. What a delinquent the aunties had turned me into — breaking into buildings, stealing, running from the cops. I had become no better than one of the Banks Brothers! And it was all the aunties' fault. "If I get caught by the cops, I'm in BIG trouble," I gasped over my shoulder.

Dotty giggled. "I was just joking, Jeremy. We were getting tired of sitting in the rain while you made up your mind what to do."

"Thanks a whole lot!" I snarled, skidding the bike to a stop. The aunties nearly fell off into a puddle, which would have served them right. "I wasn't really afraid."

"Oh?" said Gladys. "For someone who wasn't afraid, you ran off pretty smartly."

"Yeah? Well, you'd have run too if you had legs that worked," I snapped.

"The only time we run is when we snag our stockings," Dotty sighed, holding out her arm to show me a small run.

A garbage truck rumbled past, sending a spray of water over the bike and completely soaking me. The aunties snickered inside their waterproof ponchos.

Fortunately, my mother was still out on her errands when we arrived home. I got the aunties out of their ponchos and settled them on the couch. Then I brought in the box of money, which was a little damp, and shoved it back under the couch.

"I hope you're all happy, now," I said. "The money's back, just like before, and we're in a whole lot of trouble. So what do we do next?"

Gladys grinned. "Just imagine how dull your life would be without us."

"I wish you'd dry up," I said, wiping my soaking hair with a cushion.

"I wish I could," Gladys said, "dry up." She took out her handkerchief and dabbed at her rain-spattered chest. "I can almost feel the mildew coming on. I have no wish to grow mould before my time."

I could have lent her my mother's hair blower, but she didn't deserve any favours.

"I never wanted this money," I reminded them,

"and I don't want it now. *I* am not a thief! I think we should just put it all out in the garbage and forget about it."

"Our garbage has already been picked up," Dotty said, looking out the window.

I opened our damp supply bag. "Anyone else want a chocolate bar?"

The aunties refused politely, though Gladys watched every bite I took.

"Well, we've got to do *something* !" I said, finally. "Why don't you have a plan when we need one?"

"We do," Gladys said. "Wait for the Banks Brothers to find us, then capture them, and turn them and the stolen money over to the police for a big fat reward."

"Fat chance!" I said. "Figure the odds. The Banks Brothers would be a lot more likely to take us captive."

"We must get them before they get us," Gladys said in an eerie voice.

"I really think the time has come to tell someone about everything," I said. "Maybe we should tell my mom. Or confess everything to the cops and be done with it."

"And give up our chance to capture the Banks Brothers? I'm ashamed of you, Jeremy," Gladys said. "Here we were thinking you were a real man.

And what are you? A mouse."

"I have another idea," I cried. "Why not just mail the money back to the bank anonymously?"

"Always assuming you could remove your fingerprints from each bill you touched," Mabel remarked. "I just want to get rid of it," I sighed. I bit into the second chocolate bar.

"So burn it," Gladys said. "Spoil all our plans."

"This is the twentieth century," I reminded them. "You can't just go around setting fires in your backyard."

"We have a prejudice against fire anyway, don't we, girls?" Dotty said. "But what if your mother finds the money under the couch? Perhaps we should find a better hiding place."

"You'll have to think fast. My mother will be home any time. She said she was just getting groceries and going to the bank."

"That's it!" Gladys shouted. "The bank!"

"The perfect hiding place," Dotty agreed. "But can we get it in there?"

"Jeremy could," Mabel said.

I stared at them. "What are you talking about? If you think I'm going to take the risk of depositing all that money in my own bank acount, you must be nuts!"

"Not *that* bank, wet-brain," Gladys said. "*This*

one." She punched a couch cushion with a chubby finger.

"I have no idea what you're talking about."

"Have you forgotten that this very couch on which we sit is the place in which you keep your money?" Mabel replied. "If we can guard *your* money, surely we can guard *this* money."

"Put some in each of the three cushions," Dotty said. "That should even it out so the couch won't look too lumpy."

I munched the third chocolate bar and considered the aunties' plan.

"Okay," I said finally. "It's not a bad idea." I took what remained of my own money out of the couch and transferred it to Mabel's purse, so I wouldn't get it mixed up with the stolen money. I only had seventeen dollars and twenty-seven cents left. I stuffed the stolen money into the foam padding of the three couch cushions, smoothing out the lumps as best I could. I took the empty cardboard box out to the garage. Finally, I arranged the aunties back on the couch, and not even my mother could have guessed that anything in the room was different.

I flopped down, exhausted, and ate the last chocolate bar.

"It's not bad being a guard when you can sit down on the job," Dotty said.

"We are not holding up a bank," Gladys joked, "we are holding *down* a bank."

"I don't know how you can make jokes when you're sitting on a time bomb." I was still having second thoughts about the whole scheme. "What if the Banks Brothers show up here? Then there'll be trouble. All of this is *your* fault, remember. I really don't know how I got mixed up in all this."

"You made us. Remember?" Mabel said drily.

It was true. But why did it feel more like they had made me? Into someone I was not sure I wanted to be. I had become a thief, a burglar, a helpless servant of three old women who weren't even real. They strangled cops, dealt in stolen money, and sat around hoping criminals would come to visit. And to think that I had helped make them. Things were totally out of control.

"You don't seem to realize the danger you've —"

"What is done is done," said Mabel.

"Yeah, so sit on it, Jeremy," Gladys said.

I glared at them. "*You* sit on it!"

"We are," they giggled. "We are."

Dotty picked up the remote and flicked the TV on.

"Oh, no!" Gladys cried. "The only thing worse than an episode of 'Real Men/Ideal Men' is a rerun of 'Real Men/Ideal Men.'"

It was the show on friendship.

"We can tell you more about friendship than that silly announcer," Mabel said, flicking the show off.

"Sure," I said. "You can tell me about *ruining* a friendship."

"I suppose you refer to Rick," said Gladys. "You cannot keep blaming us for all your problems, dear boy."

"True friendship can survive a quarrel," Mabel said. "I am sure that Rick still wants to be friends with you as much as you want to be friends with him."

"Real friends have to trust each other and share things," I said. "They can't keep secrets from each other — like you make me keep yours!"

The aunties exchanged glances. Dotty whispered something to Mabel and Gladys. All three of them looked very guilty.

"What's going on with you three *now* ?" I asked. "Another secret? See! No wonder we can't be friends. I can't trust you for one minute!"

CHAPTER FIFTEEN

MY BRILLIANT IDEA

THE NEXT FEW DAYS were terrible. I was afraid to be in the house and afraid to leave it in case the Banks Brothers showed up. I felt like a prisoner and guard rolled into one. Daytime wasn't so bad. I even went out occasionally for a bike ride, but never for longer than five minutes. I figured the Banks Brothers would probably show up at night. Every night I would lie in bed listening for the sounds of a break-in and gunshots, planning how I would race into the bathroom and lock the door . . . But a bathroom lock wouldn't stop the Banks Brothers. And what if they shot my mother? What if I slept through it all and woke up dead in my bed? I began to wonder if I was one hundred per cent sane. I was a nervous wreck. It was all the aunties' fault. They refused to tell me what their plan was for capturing the Brothers.

"You worry too much," they said. "Everything is under control. We hope."

They did not help matters with their suggestion that I might feel better if I had a doll.

"A what?" I said.

Gladys chuckled. "A Jeremy doll."

"Mabel is an excellent seamstress," Dotty said. "You get her some stuffing and some of your clothes and things, and she'll stitch up a perfect likeness of you."

"For your own protection," Gladys added. "Just in case, you know."

"In case of what?" I stared at them. "W-wait a minute. You want to make a doll just like me, so that if — something happens — I'll turn into a ghost like you?" The aunties had it all backwards. I had made them. They couldn't make me.

"Step this way," said Mabel, "so I can take your measurements."

"But this doll idea would only work if I, uh, died right here in the living room, wouldn't it?" I shivered, imagining the Banks Brothers firing a shot through the window. "And anyway, what about a photo? Doesn't all this have something to do with those little tintypes? Forget it. No deal. No doll. I'll take my chances being real."

"Can't you appreciate a joke, Jeremy?" They all laughed. "Don't worry so much. We've got everything all figured out. Trust us."

Sure.

Every morning I got up early to watch the news, hoping I would hear that the police had caught the

Banks Brothers. After a particularly sleepless night I decided I had had enough. I could not stand the thought of that money in the couch cushions a day longer. I had to make the aunties share their plan with me.

"Up so early?" My mother was sitting in an armchair in her housecoat, with a plate of waffles and a notepad. How could I talk to the aunties with my mother sitting there?

"You know, you're looking awfully pale these days, Jeremy," my mother commented. "Maybe you should have a checkup with Dr. Suggs."

I did feel sick when I thought about the Banks Brothers finding me. I'd been losing so much sleep over it, no wonder I was pale.

My mother sighed. "I suppose all this peculiar solitary behaviour you've been exhibiting lately is actually normal for a boy your age. Why don't you have Rick over anymore? Oh, you're growing up so fast. I bet some of your friends are already dating. Maybe what you need to snap you out of your loneliness is a girlfriend? You seem far too young for a girlfriend to me, Jeremy, but —"

"A girlfriend? No way!" Girls! I had more than enough trouble with the four I shared the house with. Why had I ever thought my mother was easy to talk to?

She sighed again. "You're at a difficult age . . . You're so moody lately, and stubborn. You're turning into a young man, Jeremy. I suppose it's difficult for you to adjust."

I was ready to slam out of the room. I had had enough of that Real Man teasing from the aunties. But just then I thought of a way to get *her* out of the room.

"Hey," I said, "the smell of those waffles gives me a real appetite. How about one of your porridge-yoghurt shakes to go with them?" I smacked my lips. "You know, the nutritious kind with wheatgerm and raw egg?"

She narrowed her eyes. "I thought you hated my oatmeal shakes. Last time you fed yours to the neighbour's cat. You *must* be sick, Jeremy."

"I'm fine," I insisted. "Just a little tired, that's all."

"If you're tired, why are you up so early?"

"Um, just thought I'd watch the news."

"That's another thing," she said. "This business of having the TV on all the time. Do you think I haven't noticed that it's on nearly all day every day?" She went out to the kitchen to whip up one of her ghastly slimy porridge shakes. "And by the way," she called, "you still owe me twenty-nine bucks for the aunties' new clothes. Haven't you got the reward cheque yet? The cops are taking long enough to get it to you."

I realized I had never told her the sad news. I would have to mow at least three or four lawns to pay her back for those dumb old new clothes.

Mom returned with the oatmeal shake, and I had to force it down, acting as if I enjoyed it while she watched.

She spent most of the day in the living room with her notepad, so I couldn't talk to the aunties. Maybe the time had come to tell my mother the whole story. I was sure she would believe me. That wasn't the problem. Or rather, that *was* the problem. She would immediately invite all her friends to come and hear about it. The aunties would be furious. They might never speak to me again. Telling my mother would only make things worse. And it would not stop the Banks Brothers from coming.

"What are you doing with that notepad?" I asked her.

She put down her pen. "Well, since I'm out of a job now, I thought I'd try my hand at a little writing. You know, with my imagination . . ."

"Really? Newspaper articles? A TV series? Kids' books?"

"Horror. Yes, I think I'd be quite good at horror drama. It probably pays well too. And we sure could use the money."

If only my mother knew how much her couch was worth.

Finally, just before supper I got a chance to talk to the aunties alone.

"If you don't tell me your plans about capturing the Banks Brothers this instant," I said firmly, "I'm going to . . . I'm going to . . ."

"You're going to what, Jeremy?" Dotty asked sweetly.

"Cackle cackle, bwack bwack," Gladys clucked. "What are you, a chicken?"

"You need something to take your mind off your worries," Mabel said. "Perhaps," she added, in a perfect imitation of my mother's voice, "perhaps what you need is a girlfriend."

I left the three of them chuckling on the couch and went for supper. We had chicken. It tasted odd. Porridgy. I did not ask my mother what the stuffing was. I did not want to get on the subject of stuffing. Or chickens.

After supper we made popcorn and watched a movie about a guy who got lost underground and was captured by giant earthworms. I actually forgot my worries enough to relax and enjoy it. My mother spent most of the time comparing TV with live theatre.

"TV stifles the imagination," she said. "Unlike plays, or books, which force you to think."

"You watch it."

"Only the news. Which is, unfortunately, far too entertaining. Too much TV, I read recently, distorts your perception of reality. And shows like this one can give you bad dreams."

Personally, I thought the movie was pretty funny. And not half as scary as real life.

"Why are you watching it, then?" I asked.

"Because, Jeremy, I think the two of us should spend more time together. I've barely seen you this summer. We should have a game of cards, or a conversation, or hit tennis balls against the house or something. Sigh. You're growing up on me . . ."

The aunties sat on the couch behind us smugly nodding agreement. Between the four of them, they really knew how to ruin an evening.

That night I lay in bed totally exhausted. My mind was a blank. Such a blank that when I finally fell asleep I might have known I'd have another weird dream.

In my dream, the aunties and I were in a theatre, rehearsing a play late at night. The set must have been designed by my mother, because it looked exactly like our living room. There was no audience, but off in one corner a photographer was half-hidden behind an old movie camera covered with a black drape. All we could see were his legs, in green rubber hip waders, and one plaid arm, which was turning a crank on the camera.

"What are you doing here?" I asked him. "This is *my* dream. I mean, my living room. Butt out."

"Aw, shut yerr beak, laddie," he replied pleasantly. "And tell me, arre ye rreally a Rreal Man?"

"I have nothing to do with that idiotic show!"

"Me neitherr. 'Rreal Men/Ideal Men' was the worrst serries I everr had the misforrtune to film. I'm glad they fired me. But we'll show them." He patted his camera. "This film is forr a new rrival show: 'Fake Men/Shake'n'Bake Men.' It's about Chicken Men like ye. Ye'rre perrfect forr the parrt, laddie. I'll be noting it in me diarry. Good show. Cheerrio!"

He packed up his camera and disappeared.

I woke up with a brilliant idea!

It was so simple I was amazed I hadn't thought of it before. There was a very easy way to prove to Rick that the aunties could talk. Fergus Phillips had come to me in my dream and given me the answer. Home movies! Rick had a camcorder. I could invite him to hide out in the hall and film me talking to the aunties in the living room. When the aunties saw and heard themselves on TV they would no longer be able to pretend to Rick that they were just stuffed dolls. With Rick knowing their secret, the aunties would have to smarten up. They wouldn't be able to boss two of us around like they had just me. I was killing myself laughing, thinking how much fun it would be watching the aunties on a video. They would be the actors and I would sit there making sarcastic comments right in front of them. They'd ruined lots of shows for me.

I dialled Rick's number. It was great to think that at last we would be friends again. The camcorder would put an end to our argument over the aunties. I would tell Rick everything, and together we could figure out what to do about the Banks Brothers.

"Ricketts here," he said.

"It's Jeremy!" I announced.

"Oh, hi. I'm glad you called."

"You are?"

"Yeah. I've been thinking about calling you."

"You have?"

"Yeah. There's a party on at our place tonight. I wanted to invite you, but I thought you might say no."

"Oh," I said slowly.

"Can you make it?"

It sounded great. I knew my mother was going. But that meant the aunties would be left all alone. Maybe that would serve them right. But somebody had to stay and guard the house.

"Gee, I'd really like to," I said. "*Really* like to. But I can't. Not unless you can come over this afternoon with your camcorder and —"

"I can't. I've got to help my dad get ready for the party. What do you need my camcorder for? I thought my telephone answering machine would do the trick."

"What are you talking about?" I asked.

"Never mind. What are *you* talking about?"

"I can't explain," I said. "I want to but — can't. Tomorrow, when the party's over, can you please come to my place with your camcorder? I can't explain now, but I'll be able to tell you everything then, I promise." I knew I must sound rude and ridiculous.

But Rick didn't sound mad, just disappointed, and said he would come the next day.

All day I went around feeling pretty clever that I had a secret the aunties didn't suspect. At the same time I felt pretty worried that I still didn't know how to stop the Banks Brothers from coming to get their money. The aunties seemed preoccupied with their own thoughts and rudely paid me no attention at all.

Around eight o'clock that night, my mother paused on her way through the hall and glanced into the living room, where the aunties and I were reading. The aunties immediately started pretending they weren't. I knew I'd have to be more careful. If I let them sit there with *Reader's Digests* in their hands, my mother would soon start suspecting they were real. Or that I was crazy. She stared at us for a few seconds. She was probably examining me for signs of mental illness.

"You know," she said finally, "I think I have figured out your problem, Jeremy. Your guilty secret."

"What?" I felt myself go hot and cold. I had so many secrets I couldn't even guess which one she had figured out. The aunties looked worried too.

"I've been wondering why you spend so much time in here alone," she went on, "and now I think I know."

I held my breath.

"At first I thought it was the aunties, but now I know the real reason."

"W-w-what do you mean?"

"You, Jeremy, are a television addict!"

I couldn't keep from laughing.

"It's not a laughing matter," she said. "You'll watch anything. Look, you've got the silly thing turned on even when you're reading. It's on all the time. The other day you watched the news *all day long* ."

"It's important to keep up with things," I mumbled.

"But you're missing life, Jeremy! You have become an observer of the lives of characters who are not even real people. The ultimate couch potato. You spend too much time here all alone. You really should get out more. Find a friend, join a hockey team, have some fun. *Live* a little. I don't understand why you aren't coming to the party tonight."

I shrugged. "If you don't hurry, you'll be late."

"I'm just concerned that your life is too dull for a boy your age. I mean, here I am, heading out for a wild party with my friends, and here you are, spending a quiet evening at home. There's something wrong there somewhere, don't you agree?"

I shrugged again.

"Oh, Jeremy, I'm not trying to run your life for you. But I don't want you to grow up lonely and bored with life."

"I'm not, Mom, honest. Don't worry about me. I'll be fine." I hoped I sounded convincing.

"I don't really like to go out and leave you alone at night, but I guess you're old enough to look after yourself. Maybe I worry about you too much. It's only because I love you so much, Jeremy . . . If you change your mind about coming, phone me and I'll come and pick you up." She kissed me good-bye and hugged me so tight it almost brought tears to my eyes.

I listened to the farewell tooting of the horn as she reversed out of the driveway and squealed around the corner. If only I could have gone with her . . .

"I hope you realize, Jeremy," Mabel said, carefully putting a bookmark in her Digest, "that your dear mother is absolutely right. Your life is too dull for a boy your age."

"Too dull? Are you kidding? My life is terrifying. Thanks to you three!"

"You need some excitement," Gladys said. "How about our own party? The three of us were made to party, weren't we, girls?"

I suddenly remembered my idea of filming the aunties for a TV video, and cheered up slightly. A party might be a good way to celebrate the last day the aunties would be able to boss me around.

"Maybe you're right for a change," I said. "We might as well have some fun. Let's party!"

CHAPTER SIXTEEN

A PETRIFYING PIZZA PARTY

I DIALLED UP A PIZZA PLACE downtown that delivered to the door and ordered a twelve-slice deep-dish double cheese Hawaiian ham and pineapple deluxe specialissimo with olives. I ignored the aunties' comments about indigestible food and got out chips, peanuts, and ginger ale. So what if the aunties didn't eat? What was a party without food?

We played a few rounds of Snap, which was their favourite game, though they were pretty slow and clumsy at putting down the cards. I won every round. It put me in such a good mood I decided to tell them about the old photographer's diary.

"There's something I haven't told you about," I began.

"You have been keeping something from us, young man?" Gladys interrupted. "After all we've done for you? I call that most ungrateful."

"You're not the only ones with secrets." I grinned, thinking of Rick's video camera.

"Making plans without us," Dotty said sadly. "He simply can't be trusted."

"*I* can't be trusted! I'm the only trustworthy

person in this room! All these weeks I've kept your secret! I haven't told a soul! Doesn't that count for anything with you?"

"Big deal," said Gladys. "What if you *had* told someone about us? It wouldn't have made a speck of difference. We would simply refuse to talk to anyone else. Not even if they tickled us to death. If you told our secret you would only end up looking silly."

I just smiled a secret smile.

"How can we trust you when you almost sold me to Rose's second-hand shop?" Dotty asked with a catch in her voice. "We mean no more to you than, than . . ."

"If anyone in this room can't be trusted," I said, "it's you three, not me. When I first met you I thought you were honest, but now I can't trust you an inch! You've tricked me, and got me into trouble, and now you're risking my life and my mother's just for the sake of excitement. Breaking into buildings, stealing money, hiding from the law! You're the most dishonest and wicked old women I've ever met! You're no better than the Banks Brothers!"

The aunties seemed truly shocked by my outburst. At last Mabel broke the silence.

"We are hurt to think that you have misunderstood us so badly, Jeremy," she said. "It is a very sad thing to be mistrusted and falsely accused. After all our adventures together, we dared to hope you were becoming fond of us. We hoped that the affection between us might one day become true friendship. We cannot deny that we have committed all the crimes you mentioned: break-and-enter, theft, conspiracy. We amazed ourselves. And yet, if you only understood that —"

The doorbell rang.

We all froze. The room was dead silent. Goosebumps sprang out all over my body.

"Well, aren't you getting the door?" Gladys asked. "You ordered a pizza."

"Oh. Right. I forgot about that." I got up and went to the front door.

No one was there.

There was a knock on the back door.

"He must have gone around the back," I said. "I'll get it." As I went to answer the back door, I thought I saw Dotty reaching for the phone. Now what was she was up to? I couldn't trust those three behind my back for one second. I flicked on the outside light and opened the back door.

In stepped Eddy Banks. Two men pushed in behind him. The oldest, a pale, white-haired man with a hearing aid and a briefcase, slammed the door shut and locked it behind them. The other one, a big man with dirty hands and a scarred face, pointed a

169

gun straight at me.

"Hello, sonny," Eddy said. "We've finally tracked you down."

I backed into the living room, too terrified to speak.

"You've got a lot of talking to do, sonny," Eddy said. "Where's the money?"

"I don't have m-much," I stammered, glancing towards the couch. "Don't shoot. Take the TV. It's worth a lot."

"Don't get funny, sonny. I've had enough of your tricks. Hand over the stash."

"Yo, Eddy. Yo, Mort," the man with the gun said. "Look at the dolls. Hey, that dame on the left looks kinda familiar. Wasn't she in the store the night we muffed the bank job?"

"Well, well, well." Eddy looked at Dotty. "I think you're right, Harv. Now how did a window dummy get from that store to this house?" He scratched his head. "Something's fishy here, eh, boys?"

Mort and Harv nodded.

Mabel cleared her throat. "Good evening, gentlemen. We have been expecting you."

The Banks Brothers gasped and drew back from the aunties, cowering around my armchair. Harv raised his gun and aimed it at Mabel.

"Don't shoot!" I yelled.

"Some people," Mabel said with dignity, "have no manners. Bursting in upon a private party. I merely wished to point out that it took you long enough to arrive."

"Sh-sh-she t-t-talks!" Eddy was white. His eyes were bulging. "Ghosts," he whispered, edging towards the door. "Keep 'em covered, Harv."

"Wait!" I cried. "I can explain everything. They're my aunties. They live here. They can't walk. They won't hurt you, don't worry. Please put your gun down, please . . ."

Eddy laughed shakily. "Ha, ha, almost fooled us into thinking you were ghosts, didn't yous. They're *real*, boys. As real as you and me. Dressed up for a costume party in stocking masks. We've used masks like that before too, eh, boys? Ha, ha. They're probably three young gals dressed up like old dames." He winked slyly at me.

"Should we trust 'em, Eddy?" Mort asked out of the corner of his mouth.

"Aw, what can three dames and little sonny here do against the three of us?" Eddy laughed.

"I see," Mabel said, "that the police have not yet tracked you down."

"We'd never have been caught in the first place if someone hadn't of squealed on us." Eddy glared suspiciously from me to Dotty.

"Don't look at me." Dotty smoothed her hair and waved her cigarette holder. "Do you think I would squeal on three handsome gentlemen like yourselves?"

Eddy grinned, then glared. "Don't change the subject," he growled. "We know you've got the money. Hand it over!" He took an angry step in my direction. "Bet you were laughing pretty hard that morning you kicked the bundle back into the river. Me thinking all the while the money was still inside it."

"I thought it *was*, honest!"

"Pretty funny money, sonny," Eddy snarled. "Made me dive down into that mud hole after a bunch of magazines wrapped up in dames' drawers!"

"Dames' what?"

"Drawers! Bloomers!" Eddy's face went red. "Underpants!"

Gladys snorted with laughter. Dotty giggled. Mabel could not hide a smile.

"Cut that out!" he yelled. "Quit your cackling! Dry up!"

That set the aunties laughing even harder. In spite of my fright, I began to giggle too, and soon the four of us were nearly rolling on the floor. Eddy grabbed the gun from Harv and pointed it at us.

"You got two minutes to tell us where you put

the money," he snarled. "Or *else*."

"Lower that pistol," Mabel ordered grandly, "or we shall tell you nothing."

Eddy lowered the gun an inch or two. Mabel calmly folded her gloves.

"First of all," she began, "Jeremy knew nothing about the money. So you must not blame him. Dotty and Gladys and I take full responsibility. As you may or may not know," she went on, "the four of us were responsible for your first arrest. We could not help but take it as a personal insult when you had the poor manners to evade justice. We deduced what occurred when you escaped by motorcycle and had an accident by the bridge. We were successful in recovering the money from the river using fish hooks.

Jeremy knew nothing of our plans to keep the money as bait to recapture you," she continued. "He insisted on returning it to the fishing hole. While he was out of the room, the three of us hid the money from the tin box and replaced it with magazines. We muffled them up in a pair of, er, unmentionables — donated by Gladys."

"Just a little touch of humour," Gladys explained.

"What?" I asked in amazement. "How did Gladys get her, her, uh, underwear off by herself?" Could they move more than I realized? Were they

174

pretending to be a lot more helpless than they really were?

"When your mother dressed us in new outfits, she put all our old clothes in a box under the couch," Mabel reminded me. "Gladys dragged it out with her umbrella." She looked as though she was trying to wink at me.

"Forget the details," Eddy roared. "Where's the loot?"

"Hidden," Mabel said proudly.

"We'll find it," Eddy said. The three brothers moved menacingly towards the couch.

Just as the Banks Brothers were about to grab the aunties, the telephone rang. I reached to pick it up.

Eddy whirled and pointed the gun. "Let it ring! They'll think they dialled the wrong number."

It was nearly eleven. Who would be calling so late? Maybe Rick! Maybe he had changed his mind and decided to come over . . . which might not be the greatest idea at the moment. I sighed. It was probably just the pizza place checking the address.

"It might be Jeremy's mother," Dotty said. "If Jeremy doesn't answer she'll think something is wrong." The phone kept ringing.

"Okay," Eddy snarled, pointing the gun at Gladys. "You. Pick up the phone and tell them they got the wrong number. Then leave it off the hook so they get a busy signal next time."

Gladys reached across the coffee table and clumsily picked up the phone. "Hello?" she said into the wrong end of the receiver. "Hello? Hello? There's no answer," she whispered. "Maybe it's one of those calls where people whisper nasty things at you."

"Quit fooling!" Eddy hissed. "Turn that receiver the right way around."

"She doesn't know any better," I tried to explain. "She's never talked on the phone before."

"Oh yes I have!" Gladys said. "I mean, well, I mean I . . ."

By this time we could all hear an anxious voice on the other end of the line — my mother's. "Jeremy? Are you there? Jeremy, what's going on?"

I looked at Eddy. He was sweating.

"Okay, talk to her," he growled. "But no false moves." He levelled his gun. "I got Black Boomer pointed right at your cake hole."

I picked up the phone with shaking fingers. The three Banks Brothers and the three aunties leaned forward to listen.

"Hello?" I said into the mouthpiece. "Yes. Sure. No. I could hardly hear you — must have been a bad connection." Eddy nodded approvingly.

"What? No, really, Mom, I'm not bored here by

myself. Uh-huh. Sure. Fine. Yes. Uh-huh. No." The aunties were glaring at me. I hoped the conversation was not offending Eddy. Out of the corner of my eye I could see Black Boomer moving closer. "Yes, see you later," I said into the phone. "No, no, I'm in the middle of a show. What? Oh" — I glanced nervously at the gun — "sort of a suspense drama, I guess. No, Mom, I'm not s-scared. Enjoy your party. Bye."

"Good bluffing, sonny," Eddy said. "You got the makings of a real criminal. Now, to work. If the loot's in this house, we're gonna find it." He laid the gun on the coffee table and each of the brothers roughly grabbed an auntie.

I threw myself out of my chair, scattering a bowl of chips and a stack of magazines, and grabbed the gun.

CHAPTER SEVENTEEN

CLOSETPHOBIA

BEFORE I REALIZED what I had done, I found myself waving Black Boomer at the brothers' backs.

"One false move and I'll blow your gizzards to Shanghai," I snarled. Those Banks Brothers weren't going to touch my aunties.

"Good gracious, Jeremy, put that dreadful weapon down this instant!" Dotty ordered. "You could hurt someone."

"Reach for the sky," I said softly, moving the gun slowly in front of the Banks Brothers. Maybe I *was* cut out to be a criminal. It all came so naturally.

"Hand me that gun at once, Jeremy," Gladys said. "I am shocked at your behaviour."

"Thinkin' hard, sonny?" Eddy looked pretty silly with his arms up in the air. "What are you going to do? Call the cops? Shoot us?"

Of course he knew I wouldn't call the cops. And I wouldn't shoot, either.

"Are we all gonna wait here till Momma comes home?" Harvey asked.

"I just want you to leave," I said, sounding a hundred times calmer than I felt "Just go away and leave us alone."

"You're scared to shoot us, aren't you, sonny?" Eddy smiled. "So what if we won't go? Do we look scared? Eddy, Mort, and Harvey Banks aren't scared of nothin', sonny. 'Cept ghosts, maybe. Ha ha."

I pinched myself, although I knew this was no dream. I glared at the aunties. Just how had they planned to capture the Banks Brothers? It looked as if they had no plan after all.

"Well, gentlemen," Mabel said sadly, "I suppose you win. We will give up the money if you promise to leave."

Eddy grinned. "Promise."

"We accept your promise," Mabel said. "Now then, Jeremy, please give the Banks Brothers the couch cushions."

"Ha! I figured the money was in there." Eddy stepped forward, but stopped when he noticed I had Black Boomer aimed at his gizzard.

The aunties did have a plan! They would let the Brothers have the cash and I would keep them covered with their own gun while I phoned the cops. When the cops arrived I could make up some story about how the Brothers had burst into my house and tried to take me hostage while they demanded a get-away helicopter to fly to Phoenix, Arizona . . . I could tell the cops anything! They would believe my story rather than the robbers'. I was almost grinning as I moved the aunties off the couch and handed each brother a cushion.

Then Mabel said, "And Jeremy, please give Mr. Banks his gun."

"What? Now? No way!" It would spoil the whole plan if I gave up Black Boomer. Eddy would shoot me deader than a dodo the second he had the gun back in his hand.

"Violence," Mabel said severely, "is never an acceptable form of behaviour. We must guard against sinking to the criminal level in times of stress." She turned to the brothers, who were eagerly unzipping the cushions and stuffing handfuls of hundred-dollar bills into Mort's briefcase.

Gladys, who was nearest me, grabbed the gun out of my hands.

"Please take the proceeds of your criminal activities out of our cushions and leave at once," Mabel said. "There is no need to thank us for safeguarding your money for you. We do not wish to be embarrassed by your gratitude." She looked very dignified as she finished her speech.

Dotty gave them her sweetest smile and Gladys looked respectful.

"Sure, ma'am, you bet. We got some manners left, eh, boys? We ain't out to hurt three dames and a little boy. You're a real lady, ma'am, even if you do dress up in funny duds. Nice to meet yous all. Well, guess we'll hit the road. We got Black Betty parked just around the corner." He held out his hand.

Gladys slowly drew the gun from her lap and passed it to him.

"Don't be a fool!" I squeaked. "He'll shoot! Crooks don't keep promises!" I closed my eyes, waiting for the shot. When I opened them a few seconds later to check what the delay was, the gun was tucked into Eddy's belt and the brothers were heading for the door. I felt weak.

"Hey!" Harvey said suddenly. "Was that a car stopping outside? Cops! Run for it, boys!"

"I never called them. Honest!" I stuck my hands into the air.

"Use the back door," Mabel advised them.

The Banks Brothers raced for the back hall, Mort clutching the briefcase full of money. Harv knocked over a lamp. A door slammed. We heard a muffled cry from the hall, and a confusion of terrified Banks voices. "Aaagh! Help! Where are we? The door's stuck! We're trapped!" There was a sound of things like tennis raquets and skates and boots falling.

"It is not the police," said Mabel, who could see out the window from the armchair I had moved her to. "It is just an ordinary blue car."

"The pizza man, at last." Gladys was laughing so hard she could hardly talk. "Three simpletons scared away by the pizza-pie man. Trapped in the closet! Haw, haw, haw!"

"So much for your plans!" I said. "You would have let them get away, money and all. It's only by accident they're stuck in the closet. They're safe enough for the moment. It's pretty impossible to open that door from the inside. *Now* what do we do? And that was a dumb risk, giving Eddy's gun back," I told Mabel in a shaky voice. "They could have killed us all!"

"A gun, my dear Jeremy, is illegal and immoral, and is even more difficult to get rid of than stolen money," Mabel replied. "Besides, I assumed you would have the presence of mind to remove the bullets while I was distracting them. You did, I hope."

I blushed. I had no idea how to take bullets out of a gun. I'd have likely shot my hand off.

"Don't worry," Gladys grinned. "*I* removed the bullets." She pointed to the little pile in her lap.

A car door slammed in the driveway.

"If that's the police, they're late," Dotty said. "And if it's not, we had better redial."

"What are you talking about?" I asked. A

hesitant tapping came from the hall closet door. I glanced at the aunties, then went over and put my ear to the crack.

"Pst, pst? Sonny?" Eddy whispered. "You out there, sonny?"

"Yeah, whaddaya want?"

"Sonny, was that the cops who drove up or what?"

"It's only the pizza man, scaredy! Ha, ha!"

"*Then let us outta here!*" Eddy shouted. "All three of us are closetphobic. That means we're allergic to small spaces. That's why we can never stay in jail cells too long. Let us out!"

"Oh, shut up," I said. "I've got some thinking to do."

The doorbell rang, and a voice on the other side of the door said sternly, "Police. Open up."

"Did you hear that?" I whispered.

"The pizza man must have a strange sense of humour," Gladys replied, still chuckling.

"What should I do?"

"You are on your own now," Mabel said. "We do not talk, remember? Especially not to the police."

I turned the knob slowly and opened the door a crack.

Two people stood on the front porch. They were not wearing police uniforms. I recognized them anyway.

"We'd like a few words with you," the man said.

"How do I know you're really the police?" I held tightly to the door, stalling for time.

"Oh, for pity's sake, you know perfectly well who we are," the woman said. "Come on, Roddy — I mean Constable Heaves — show the little smart-aleck your identification."

The red-haired man flicked out his badge. "Constable Rodney Heaves and my partner, Constable Sheila Barflie. Don't pretend you don't know who I am, kid. I'm the one who caught you jay-riding in front of the old clothes store. I'm the one you flagged down that morning the Banks Brothers pulled the bank job. Of course you know me."

"And you know *me* from that day you were trespassing by the river and nearly strangled poor Roddy," Sheila said. "We're here to investigate a complaint about noise. Someone phoned and reported a loud party going on here."

"You must have the wrong address," I said. Were the aunties up to some trick? I remembered Dotty reaching for the phone. But there had been no time for her to have called the police.

"Funny the way your name always seems to come up whenever we're getting close to the Banks

184

Brothers," Rod said. "Earlier tonight we had a report of a stolen black van spotted in this neighbourhood. I am suspicious of coincidences."

"Me too," I said in a small voice.

"Sounds like the kid's got something to hide," Rod told Sheila. "Or some*one*. Let's take a look."

They pushed their way inside.

I was shaking. There was no sound from the closet.

"U-u-u-um," I stuttered. My heart was in my mouth. Three robbers were trapped in my hall closet and I had had no time to think up a story. I didn't know what to do. Tell the cops? Would they believe me? If only I could ask the aunties, but of course they would never speak in front of the police.

"It looks like a cyclone hit this place." Sheila stared into the living room.

I had to agree it did look worse than usual, with the aunties sprawled around, the couch cushions unzipped on the floor, a lamp knocked over, and chips and magazines scattered everywhere.

"Having a little tea party with your dolls, I see," Sheila commented, and added in a low voice, "I told you the kid's odd, Roddy."

"Looks like a break-in to me," Rod said. "Had some unexpected visitors tonight, did you?"

I set the lamp back on the table and shook my

head. "N-no one broke in," I stammered. That was true. The Banks Brothers had knocked and I'd *let* them in. "You're the only unexpected visitors tonight."

Another car door slammed in the driveway.

"My mother!" I cried. "Oh, no!" How would I ever explain the big mess and the two police constables in the living room? There was no time to think of a story. No matter what I said, both my mother and the cops would get suspicious. I slumped into a chair and put my head in my hands.

CHAPTER EIGHTEEN

JEREMY, RICK, AND THE AUNTIES

THE DOORBELL RANG. Mabel, beside me, gave me a poke with her cane and tried to whisper something. I glared at her, warning her with my eyes not to make things even worse by suddenly speaking.

"You look sick, kid," Rod said. "Shall I get the door?"

And Sheila said, "Does your mother usually ring at her own front door?"

I jumped up. Of course! My mother had her keys. I almost laughed with relief, and did not even stop to wonder who else it might be.

"OnetwelveslicedeepdishdoublecheeseHawaiian hamandpineappledeluxespecialissimo pizza? With olives?" said the pizza man as I opened the door.

Behind him my friend Rick was just hopping off his bike. He raced to the door, panting.

"Is that blue car in the drive a cop car?" he asked breathlessly. "What's going on?"

"Shh," I hissed. "What are you doing here?"

"I'm delivering a pizza?" the pizza man said. "Maybe I have the wrong address?"

"No, it's the right address. Come in."

Rick and the pizza man went into the living room. The cops looked them up and down suspiciously.

Behind me I heard a faint sawing sound, as if someone was trying to cut through a door with a skate blade.

It was a little embarrassing paying for the pizza. With everyone looking on, I took my money out of Mabel's purse.

"Cute purse you've got there," the pizza man said. I did not give him a tip.

After the pizza man left I frantically tried to think what to do next. Should I turn the Banks Brothers in and take my chances getting arrested along with them? I glanced at the aunties, but they just sat there like three stuffed dolls. I felt I owed it to them not to do anything before I'd discussed it with them. That meant getting rid of Rod and Sheila.

I held out the pizza box. "I would like to offer you this little pizza," I babbled, "since you had to waste your evening coming over here for no reason at all. I hope you don't mind olives. You should eat it while it's still hot." I glanced meaningfully at the front door.

"No reason?" Rick interrupted. "What about the Banks Brothers? You mean they got away with the money? I thought . . ."

My mouth fell open. My shoulders dropped. I put my head in my hands again.

"All right," Rod said, "let's have the truth here. Just what do you boys know about the Banks Brothers?"

"You'd better tell him everything, Jeremy," Rick said.

Some friend! Giving me up to the cops just as I was about to get rid of them. And yet, I couldn't help thinking it would be a relief to tell the truth and get it all over with. I glanced nervously at the aunties, and began.

"Well," I said, "well, it kind of made me mad when I caught the Banks Brothers before and the cops wouldn't give me the reward. So —" I glanced at the aunties again, "so if I wanted the reward I knew I would have to catch the Banks Brothers again. Although I didn't really plan to. I heard the news report about the motorcycle accident by the bridge and uh, one way or another figured out what must have happened. I went to the fishing hole, and, uh, caught Constable Heaves by mistake, and then I snagged a soggy old bundle by mistake. I took it home, having no idea it was actually the stolen money."

"Your story's full of holes," Sheila scoffed. "It doesn't hold water."

"I spent three days in that scummy river looking for the money," Rod said. "Do you mean to tell me you had it all the time? That's possession of stolen property. I could take you in!"

"Please don't," I said. "I honestly never meant to take that money. I can explain everything."

I tried my best. The story got harder and harder as I went along because I had to keep the aunties out of it, for their own protection as well as mine.

"Well, you know the Banks Brothers were watching that fishing hole. They must have seen me hook the bundle, and somehow they must have tracked me down."

"You expect us to believe that line?" Sheila snorted. "I've heard some real fish stories before, but this is one whale of a tale. If you think we're going to swallow it hook, line, and sinker, you've missed the boat."

I decided to ignore her.

"And so," I concluded, "the Banks Brothers found me, but I managed to get their gun, and it's not loaded anymore, and they are now trapped in the hall closet with all the money."

"*What?*" gasped Rod, Sheila, and Rick all together.

I nodded. "Go see for yourselves, if you don't believe me. Here, you can have the bullets from their gun. I don't want them."

"Get the handcuffs ready," Sheila told Rod, "just in case that slippery little eel is telling the truth."

"Trust me," I grinned, congratulating myself on having told the story without telling a single lie. Even if I had left a few details out.

Rick and I followed Rod and Sheila into the hall. There was no sound from the closet.

"You sure you were working alone?" Rod said suddenly. "You sure you didn't have a little help on this?"

I didn't know how to answer.

"Of course he had some help," Rick said.

Oh, no! Not now! Please don't tell about the aunties!

"Artificial intelligence," Rick said. "Like computers, you know. The police should use them."

"*What?*" Rod and I asked at the same time.

"If you feed all available information into computers, you come up with all sorts of answers and interesting possibilities. That's what Jeremy did. Of course, his three are a little old, with limited memory capacity, and quite a few stitches, I mean glitches. But he couldn't have done it without their help, could you, Jeremy."

"Rick's r-right," I stammered. "Absolutely right."

"Well," said Sheila. "That makes some sense.

Why didn't you tell us that before? With technology on your side, I can see why you had an edge on us. The police department is going to have to modernize before any more criminals slip through our net."

I winked at the aunties.

It did not take long for Rod and Sheila to get Eddy and Harv and Mort and the briefcase out of the closet and bundled into the car. Rick and I followed them out to the driveway. Eddy glared at me.

"I hope you don't join the police force when you grow up, sonny," he growled. " 'Cause you'd make a first-rate robber. Look me up in a few years, eh?" He stuck out his hand. I shook it.

I grinned. "Don't bank on it."

"Move along now," Rod said. He turned to me. "I'll be calling you in to the police station tomorrow to make a statement."

"No problem," I said. "I'll bring Rick along to help me out with some of the details."

"And by the way," Sheila called, before they drove off, "thanks for the pizza."

When they were finally gone, Rick and I went back into the house.

"Thanks for coming over," I said. "What would I have done without you?"

"You were doing fine," Rick said. "Jeremy, I'm sorry I didn't believe you about the aunties. It sounds like I missed out on a lot. I'll never not believe you again."

"What I can't figure out," I said, "is how come you seem to know so much. And what made you come over tonight, anyway, just in time for all the action?"

"I said I'd come over tomorrow." Rick looked at his watch and grinned. "And it's tomorrow already. Seriously, I have to admit, I was tipped off. Mabel and Gladys and Dotty told me everything."

"You did?" I stared at the aunties. "When? Why? How?"

"A few days ago. Because he was part of our capture plan. We simply phoned him."

Rick nodded. "I was a little surprised to get a phone call from the aunties. They had quite a time convincing me they were really who they said they were."

"But why?" I asked them. "I thought you didn't want anyone else to know about you."

"Well," said Mabel. "We needed Rick's answering machine. And anyway, we hoped that any friend of yours would be a friend of ours."

"I don't get it. Why do all of you seem to know more about what's been going on than I do?"

"Let me explain," Rick said. "The aunties told me about keeping the money to lure the Banks

Brothers to your house. The problem was how to capture them once they got here. The phone is right on the coffee table there. They said they would call me at the first sign of danger and I, in turn, would call the cops. We decided on a noisy party complaint, in case of false alarms. We had a code to speed things up and avoid the need to talk. The aunties just had to dial my number, let it ring once, hang up, and ring once more. Very speedy. And if I was out when they called for help, my answering machine was all hooked up to relay the message to the police station."

"We did it just as the Banks Brothers were arriving tonight," Dotty said proudly. "It took us twenty-eight seconds."

"I take back all those rotten things I said about you," I told the aunties. "What a great plan. I'm impressed!"

Mabel made the fuzzy sound that meant she was clearing her throat. "We have no complaints about you either, dear boy. Well done."

"Oh, Jeremy," Dotty cried, "you are so brave and loyal and honest and true."

"I hate to admit it," Gladys said, "but young Jeremy seems to be the closest thing to the Ideal Man that we have ever met."

"Or created," Mabel remarked.

"He thinks he made us," Gladys whispered loudly to Rick. "But it's really the other way around." They all laughed.

I blushed, and scowled. "Oh, very funny!" I said. "Very, *very* funny."

"The true test of a real man is his sense of humour," Dotty said.

"We may have taught you bravery and honesty and loyalty and a few manners since our arrival," Mabel said, "but you are still the same old gullible youngster we first met. Never mind, even the Ideal Man must have his little weakness — to keep him real." They all snickered into their gloves.

"Just a little joke between friends," Gladys explained to Rick. "We may have got you into trouble occasionally, Jeremy, but you have to admit, we've had a lot of laughs." She reached over and began tickling me.

"Heeeelp!" I squealed. "Get your gloves off me!"

"Not on your tintype, sonny," she growled.

"No tickling!" I giggled. "Help, police!"

"By the way," Rick said, "that old photographer's diary was pretty interesting. Quite the inventor, eh?"

"You read the diary?" I asked, escaping from Gladys. "You mean you actually understand how the old guy figured out how to change photos into ghosts? All that magic stuff?" The thought made me shiver.

"Ghosts? Magic? Are you kidding? Old Fergus Phillips was trying to project the first-ever television pictures. Boy, did his experiment fail!"

"TV?" I squeaked. "He was working on the first TV photography?"

"It was all in the diary, wasn't it? I thought it would be obvious to a TV nut like yourself. He wanted to preserve the past, defy space and time — you know, project his pictures anywhere, into any-one's house. The first TV."

"You're kidding." I remembered how the TV had suddenly stopped working on the night my mother and I started making the aunties, and how it had started working again the day we finished them. I told Rick about it.

"The way I see it," he said, "the aunties must be some kind of failed experiment. Too bad Fergus wasn't around to see it happen. Instead of getting them *on* TV, he got them right through it. Some kind of strange magnetic fluke. Maybe it had something to do with their photo coming in contact with television waves fifty years later. Who knows? Maybe there *was* a little magic involved."

"A likely story," Gladys remarked.

"Failed experiment indeed," Mabel said.

"Good gracious me," said Dotty.

I felt a little guilty about the trick I had been planning to play on the aunties, secretly filming them to prove to Rick they were real. It would have been a pretty mean thing to do; I knew how much they disliked TV. It might even have been dangerous. Putting the aunties on TV might have sent them back into a time where I would never be able to see them again. I shook my head. I was being totally illogical. But I was still glad I hadn't made a movie of them behind their backs. The aunties were right: TV wasn't nearly as exciting as real life.

Dotty, who was nearest the front door, put her finger to her lips.

"Shh, I hear something!"

"Ha ha," I said. "You can't scare me that easily. I know you and your tricks."

Then I heard it too: footsteps on the front porch. After only a moment's hesitation I went over and flung open the door. I let out an enormous sigh of relief.

"Am I glad to see you!" I said.

"And I'm glad to see you too," said my mother, stepping inside and giving me a kiss on the nose. "You shouldn't have waited up. You weren't scared here all alone so late, were you? Oh, Jeremy, what a party! You should have come. All the old theatre crowd was there. And Jeremy — the most exciting thing happened! We've all decided to go together and buy back the theatre! We'll convert it to a dinner theatre. I'll get a promotion from set designing to script writing! Jeremy, it's a dream come true. I've got all sorts of ideas for using the aunties in a murder mystery dinner!" My mother noticed the living room. "Goodness! What a disaster. What on earth were you doing? Hi, Rick. I could have given you a ride if I'd known you were coming over. It's about time you two got back together. Well, I'm simply exhausted. I'm going to go straight to bed. You two have a lot of catching up to do. I assume you're staying overnight, Rick? What would you like for breakfast?"

"No oatmeal shakes!" I said. "And no frogs' legs!"

"Toast," said Rick. "We deserve a toast."

My mother grinned. "Let's hear it for friends," she said. "Everybody needs one!" She yawned and headed for the stairs, murmuring something about wild parties and middle age.

"My dears!" Dotty exclaimed. "Did you hear what Jeremy's mother said about the theatre? Putting us into plays? We'll be on the stage!"

"That would never do," Mabel said sternly. "The stage indeed. How dreadfully vulgar. Nearly as low as TV. We do not exist to entertain theatre-goers, like performing monkeys."

"It might be good for a little excitement, though," Gladys said. "Now that things have quieted down around here."

"Hey! I just thought of something!" I said.

"What?" asked Rick.

"I forgot to ask Rod and Sheila if we get the reward — for information leading to the arrest of the Banks Brothers!"

"Always assuming," Mabel said drily, "that they do not escape again on the way to the police station."

Rick groaned. "Oh, no. They better not."

"Hey," I said, "Is anybody else hungry? I've still got eight bucks left. Let's order another pizza and party all night! We've got a lot to celebrate."

THE END

*